AF663026

the Courtesans *of* Karim Street

the Courtesans *of* Karim Street

DEBOTRI DHAR

NIYOGI
BOOKS

Published by
NIYOGI BOOKS
D-78, Okhla Industrial Area, Phase-I
New Delhi-110 020, INDIA
Tel: 91-11-26816301, 49327000
Fax: 91-11-26810483, 26813830
email: niyogibooks@gmail.com
website: www.niyogibooksindia.com

Text © Debotri Dhar

Editor: Mohua Mitra
Cover Design: Dsgn Unplugged
Layout: Shashi Bhushan Prasad

ISBN: 978-93-83098-99-6
Publication: 2017

All rights are reserved. No part of this publication may be reproduced or transmitted in any form or by any means, electronic or mechanical, including photocopying, recording or by any information storage and retrieval system without prior written permission and consent of the Publisher.

The responsibility of any kind for the correctness and legality of the facts stated or opinions expressed in the book is entirely of the authors and not of the publishers. The publisher has no responsibility of any kind in regard to the same.

Printed at: Niyogi Offset Pvt. Ltd., New Delhi, India

To Pavan Varma,

for more than a decade of delightful conversations on culture and identity.

For teaching me the importance of both roots and wings.

Contents

Excerpts from a Diary

Delhi, India, 1981

Today the walled city smells of turmeric. It sits in tiny orange heaps in the courtyard...earthy, pungent, slight bitter. Last week I went to Khari Baoli, the spice market; I know all about the uses of turmeric. Other spices too, *jaiphal* and *javitri* and *zaffran*, their names rolling off my tongue like ancient Indian chants. Away from Amma's cat-eyes, Shakuntala steals a pinch of the turmeric, mixes it with milk and smears the paste over her face. In the evening, she will glow like a firefly. She runs after me, her palms a bright, laughing orange, but, as always, she cannot catch me.

Outside, the sun glowers and the sky burns a gaseous blue. Houses in gaudy colours perch one on top of another. This is Shahjahanabad, the old city built by the Mughal emperor Shah Jahan in the seventeenth century. Back then the city was surrounded by a wall, I am told, its gates ironclad and fiercely guarded by sentries night and day. Some of the gates still remain, silent and watchful. Kashmiri Gate, Ajmeri Gate, Mori Gate. Ajmeri Gate opens on to Connaught Place, the central business district of New Delhi, with its Georgian architecture modelled after the Royal Crescent of Bath. Amma loves to go to Connaught Place, to get her record player mended and to buy new records. This new city is only a few kilometres away from the old one, but to Amma, another country, another people. When they pile her into the battered Ambassador and take her on a drive along Rajpath, all the way from India Gate and past the red sandstone buildings on Raisina Hill, she is very quiet. On those days, she wears one of her good saris and hangs gold *jhumka*s from the stretched holes of her earlobes. The bright-red lipstick misses her lips entirely, but when Shakuntala moves in to correct it with the pointy tip of a handkerchief, Amma will have none of it. "*Ya Allah, Hey Bhagwan,*" she says resolutely, her kohl-lined eyes flashing, and that, as her son says, is that.

I do like New Delhi; it's well planned and decidedly spiffy. But, truth is, I prefer the untidy, impossible meanderings of the old city.

I have walked endlessly through Chandni Chowk, the main street; I have explored the ruins of the Red Fort, meandered through the Jama Masjid, hovered around the old havelis. I have eaten aloo kachori and *gajar ka halwa,* slurped on kulfi and thandai, and not fallen sick even once. I have bought boxfuls of bangles, stacking them under my bed. Yet I want more of India, more. Last week I saw a sequinned white *lehanga* in the bazar and knew I had to wear it for an evening at the embassy, but he wasn't too pleased, not even with the strand of white *bela* flowers I had tucked in my hair. He did not say anything, but he swirled his glass absently when I spoke to him. I'm afraid I am not a good wife, not for such an important man. It is such a grief I carry inside me, and cannot share with anyone. Except, perhaps, this old city.

Like me, this city is full of buried worlds; it speaks to me, it understands. At night, I see the wind blow out the hanging lamps. In the darkness I lie, amid the tinkle of ankle bells and the perfumed giggles of the courtesans. I walk about, I am restless for hours. I wait for dawn, for new excursions, for another knowing.

The lanes before me are narrow, writhing, each one a snare. Where should I go today? What should I do? I don't know. So many countries I have travelled...but it is here, in this city of shadows, that I will lose myself, and find myself. This sudden knowledge peaks inside me, pulling me out of the lingering ambiguity of last night's half-dreams, and towards the clear summer sun.

The Letter

New Jersey, USA, 2012

The tree by the library was aflame, its redgold leaves crackling in the buttery October sun. Clutching her books to her chest, Megan cut deftly through a swarm of students to look at it more closely. Five-feet seven, and in an emerald silk skirt that matched the exact colour of her eyes, she looked striking; a few heads turned as she passed.

"Burning," she whispered, getting to the tree and crushing a handful of its leaves in her palm, curious to see if they would leave a stain. Slowly, she ran her fingertips over the peeling bark: fluted, fissured, orange-cinnamon. Tilting her palm to block out the sun, she looked up at the branches, urn-shaped, scaly at the base and flaky in the upper crown, bearing a profusion of three-lobed leaves that had turned, overnight, from glossy green to red. In between the branches were triangles of sky, their edges trimmed with clouds.

It might be mid-October, but the sticky gloom of the previous months had not abated. Megan's dress was damp despite the breeze, and she could have sworn her mascara was running. Unzipping her folder, she drew out the letter and scanned its contents again.

The words on the pale sheet of paper were bold, typewritten, the 'e' slightly misshapen, the K missing half an arm.

"You are not a scholar. You are a whore, as your mother was before you, and your grandmother, and great-grandmother. Ask anyone on Karim Street."

It had arrived in the mail earlier that morning. The plain white envelope had a stuck-on label with her name and address, a Brooklyn postmark and no sender information. When she'd read the words the first time, she'd felt herself stiffen into so many knots, a knot for every word. Just about anyone could have dropped it into a letterbox in New York and waited for it to make its way to her. But who? Who could possibly do something as twisted as this?

"Hey Professor Adams!"

Megan quickly put the letter back into its envelope and looked up. One of her students from her 101 class, a lanky boy in cargo pants and a baseball cap, was waving enthusiastically at her.

"Hi there! How's it going?" she called out, flashing him her characteristically dazzling smile. And instantly regretting it, when she saw him looking like he was going to faint. As a newly-minted academic in her early thirties, Megan was well aware that the students could not possibly see her as a mother figure. Quite the contrary; she was very conscious of the effect her looks had on the boys in her class, and while she couldn't be anything less than friendly with her students, it held her back from hanging out with them as much as she would have liked to. "What did you think of the reading for today's class?" she continued, turning the conversation in a scholarly direction when he walked up to her.

He still looked dazed and at a loss for words. "I...um... did go over it, I *swear*," he said, recovering quickly. "Couldn't get a word. Like, seriously. What the hell was–sorry, I mean, what was he trying to *say*?"

Megan couldn't help grinning. "Foucault does have that effect, doesn't he? I remember when I first read *Discipline and Punish* in my sophomore year. God, it was intense, exhausting, maddening. But once you get him, it will transform the way you understand power. I promise."

"Can't wait," her student muttered dubiously. "On an unrelated note, the female can't stop gloating about the fall colours, so I'm gonna drag her to see *this* tree. You know the story, right?"

The 'female' in question must be the girl she'd often seen him with, Megan remembered. Denims, slouchy tanks, probably a freshman too. "Yes, I've heard," she said, deciding not to rise to the bait. "The first day this tree changes colour in the fall, it's supposed to cast a spell on all who see it. Right?"

"Yeah. Looks like it's on fire, and either turns your life to gold or burns it right through," he said, looking up at the branches. "So did anything weird happen to you today?"

"No," Megan lied. "Don't tell me you believe in these urban legends..."

"The female does," he quipped, watching Megan carefully and looking dismayed when she again passed on the chance to educate him on the proper ways of addressing the fairer sex.

"Okay then," Megan said wryly, noting his expression. "You guys carry on, and I'll see you all in a bit."

A few moments after he'd sprinted off, Megan took one long, last look at the tree. Then she began to walk briskly down a dun-brown, moss-edged pathway, the letter carefully concealed among her lecture notes.

Today they looked like a row of hedgehogs, quiet and beady-eyed, their little noses glued to their laptops. "See, what I don't get is why feminism has a problem with women focusing on their roles as wives and mothers," a large, freckled boy was saying. "As long as it's their own *choice*, and they are not being kept home at gunpoint by a fundamentalist state, where's the big fuss?"

"That's a great question," Megan replied, "and one that actually allows us to understand today's article by Foucault better. So let us recall the difference between sex and gender. Sex is only biological; gender, however, is social, historical, political, and it reflects the dominant ideologies of its times. And since the dominant ideology emphasises a woman's mothering and nurturing roles—"

"Women internalise this ideology and start feeling guilty if we turn our attentions too much away from the home," finished a girl with tinted blue hair, turning around from her front row seat to glare at her freckled classmate. "So while it might seem like we are *choosing* to focus on our roles as wives and mothers, what we are doing is self-policing ourselves to fall in line with the dominant ideology."

Megan nodded. "So, in reality, there may often be a fine line between what we choose and what is dictated to us by the power structures in society. And that is exactly what our author for the day Michel Foucault was trying to say about the nature of power. He says that power is complex, it moves *through* things and institutions and people rather than being forcibly imposed *upon* them by the state. So, power ceases to be a top-down thing; it plays out as micro-power in and through all of us. We are each living embodiments of power..."

"That's actually pretty cool," interjected the lanky boy who'd chatted with Megan earlier that morning. "Like, how we think we're choosing stuff, except that we really end up doing what is expected of us!"

"Well, once we are aware of the power of dominant ideologies and gender stereotypes, we can make more informed choices," Megan pointed out. "And the modern world does give women choices that were traditionally unavailable to us. For that reason, I am also a *huge* fan of modernity."

The students were nodding their heads vigorously. "So read the Foucault article again over the weekend, and this time it should make more sense," she continued, looking at her watch. "Think about the ways in which we internalise power. And don't stop at gender; think about the power hierarchies of race, class and so on." She paused and took a sip of water from her mug. "I'll see you all on Monday. Have a great weekend."

After the students had filed out, a quiet-looking girl walked across to Megan. "I really love your class, Professor Adams," she said shyly. "You always make me think."

Megan smiled. "Thank you. I'm glad you're getting something out of it."

"I want to be a qualified professional," the girl continued earnestly. "Not like my mother and sisters."

"They don't have professions?"

She shook her head. "No. Our family is very traditional. Not that the women are necessarily *unhappy* though...I mean, sometimes three generations of women will cook together in the kitchen, and we'll laugh and joke and have a great time, you know? When I see how hard the men work, and then see my guy friends, the ones for whom gender equality just means women can be professionally successful but there are no expectations for men to take on traditionally 'female' roles like cooking...see, *that*'s where I'm confused."

"I know what you mean. But don't let that discourage you!" Megan exclaimed spiritedly. "First build your own identity as a successful professional, and then if you want a partner or to start a family – and you don't have to – find one who'll share the housework and childcare with you. Easier said than done, of course.... In the public sphere, women are still paid a few cents less than the man's dollar—and for the same work, mind you. And in the private sphere, the greater burden of housework falls on them. But at least it's a goal to strive for, don't you think?"

The girl nodded. "Did you always want to be a professor?"

"Oh, absolutely," Megan replied without hesitation, thinking of the years of hard work she had put in as a graduate student at Princeton, sitting up through the night writing journal articles, wading industriously through stacks and stacks of books like a web-toed loon. "Academics is my passion. My work has always been my priority, probably at the expense of my love life, but that's fine."

"Really, Professor? To someone from my kind of background, that's pretty hard to imagine."

"I don't know if my background was all that different," Megan replied matter-of-factly, stuffing her notes into her folder. "My mother, she wrote very well...could have been a novelist, a poet, anything. But she just wasted her talents. Died early too. I didn't want that to happen to me. Always remember—you owe it to yourself to make something of your life."

Ten minutes later, Megan was heading out of the building and towards her favourite stone bench by the steps. The steps ran all the way up to the Law Faculty, its glass and chrome building glinting briskly in the sun, and then down again on the other side, to a small but popular restaurant. She had eaten there a couple of times, and she loved their rice and spicy chicken platter with robust sides of green salad and garbanzo beans. Sometimes they had live music in the little garden outside, mostly jazz, and students drank coconut water and worked on their laptops and laughed with their mouths full. It reminded her of her days at Princeton, of hanging out with Kevin on the steps of the Firestone Library. God, she missed Princeton...

She still remembered the twentieth of April, the day she'd successfully defended her Ph.D dissertation in English Literature. She, Kevin and a couple of other friends had gone out for drinks afterwards; she'd worn a party hat on her head and got completely drunk. "Just because I can," she'd babbled happily to Kevin, thrusting her chin in his face when he'd tried to stop her from having another glass of wine.

But when it came to applying for jobs, it was so late in the spring term that all positions for the coming fall had already been filled. Her father had suggested she take a year's break and apply for positions for *next* fall. But not wanting a gap in her resume, she'd doggedly persisted in job-hunting till she came across the open-rank position in Gender Studies at Newark College. Since she'd taken enough graduate courses in feminist theory and cultural studies, and since her dissertation was on American women novelists, she'd decided to give it a shot, relieved when she was one of the two candidates selected for the job talk.

"Well, at the very least, you got some practice in how to put together a good application," her father had said. "Go give your job talk; that's even more useful practice. And then we'll stop worrying and take a holiday, to the south of France maybe? Come back refreshed, and apply for positions at the Ivy Leagues."

But as it happened, Megan's job talk had gone very well and she'd been offered an Assistant Professor position. Excited and jumpy to the hilt, she'd accepted it immediately. "Why only the Ivy Leagues, Dad?" she'd asked passionately, perched on the kitchen counter and dangling her feet. "Here, most of the students are first-generation college goers. My work would be so much more meaningful, don't you think? I mean, I do understand the problems of playing white saviour, but isn't education more important than being politically correct?"

"I see your point," her father conceded. "Besides, you wouldn't just be teaching them. You'd be learning too."

"Exactly. Just that it's a lot of travel back and forth from Princeton five days a week. I think it would make more sense to just *move* to Newark."

There her father had disagreed. Newark was a high-crime city, he'd reminded her, suggesting she live in one of the safer areas of Brooklyn or the Bronx if it was the commute she wanted to avoid. But she'd made up her mind. "I want to approach this with honesty. I want to be a part of their lives," she'd said stubbornly, and move she did.

✦

That had been in August, slightly over two months ago. Today, sitting on the bench and hugging her knees together, Megan would grudgingly admit that she had perhaps been a bit hasty. But if she had to do it over, she had no doubt she would make the same decisions again. It had felt *good* teaching these students...and the campus was a cheery place besides, even more so now, with the trees slipping into their fall shades of burgundy and plum, and copper-coloured flowers in the flowerbeds, and the wind whistling through the trees.

Deciding to get a cup of coffee, Megan brushed a dry leaf off her skirt, got up and started walking towards the café across the street, only to have her internal monologue interrupted by a car's incessant honks. Looking up, she saw the man at the wheel staring at her really hard. Hawk nose, bloodshot eyes, glint of solid gold on the wrist, pronounced leer. With supreme effort, she controlled the urge to show him a feisty finger lest any of her students see her. Instead, she folded her arms protectively across her chest and kept walking, the gully on her forehead deepening when he licked his lips and leisurely looked her up and down even as the rapid pile-up of midday traffic behind him sweated and swore.

Reaching the other side of the street, Megan had a sudden flash of memory. William, whispering into her ear as they lay on his couch nibbling at each other. *Can't blame the guys. Remember that conference? You had the same effect on me, you tease.* That conversation, so harmless at the time, now sent an uncomfortable flush seeping up her neckline. *Tease.* Oh, that ridiculous letter.

She bought a latte with whole milk and an extra shot of espresso. Then, walking back to her bench, she flipped open her file and tried to focus on the lesson plans for her lecture later that afternoon. Today she would be teaching them epistemology. 'Epistemology—a theory of knowledge. What is knowledge? How do we know? How do we settle competing truth claims? And what, for that matter, is truth?'

Closing her file again, she stared stonily into the distance.

Anklets

Delhi, India, 2012

They were pure silver, with peacock motifs carved out of green stone and tiny bells strung all around. "Beautiful," Naina murmured, holding them up.

An October sun filtered through the thick tangle of leaves overhead, lighting up the anklet bells in curious shades of moss-brown and orange. The noises of the old city were all around: the honk of autorickshaws, the tring-tring of bicycles, the wail of bangle-sellers and *kabadiwallah*s, the smoky, guttural rasps of the newer factories, the metallic din of lathes. And yet, for a moment, all fell quiet, the tinkling whisper of the anklets the only reminder of the city's musical past.

"What did you tell them? Will you do the show? If you do, you can wear this *ghungroo*," said Naina's aunt. She wore her Patiala salwar tight around her ample middle, the frilly kameez ballooning over her backside like an upturned sack of wheat. The carefully applied foundation might have concealed the bags under her eyes, were it not for her suspiciously black hair that invited one to look more closely. But her kohl-rimmed eyes were still those of a young girl: sparkling, expectant.

"I don't want to get sucked into that world again, Bua," Naina sighed, handing the anklets back to her aunt. "All that politics."

Her aunt spat a glob of betel-juice in the courtyard. "There is politics everywhere, *ladki*! Even if that good-for-nothing boy had married you, and you'd lived like a queen in his fancy house and never had to do a day's work again, even then there would have been politics. With your in-laws, your neighbours, your servants, even your husband himself!"

"You know I don't dance anymore," Naina said quietly. "I haven't worn a *ghungroo* for more than two years now...I am completely out of practice."

"Nonsense! You are the best dancer in this city," her aunt countered, eyes like cinders. "So what if you have only done five group performances and one solo? Didn't you get noticed every single time? Or else why would those good-for-nothing reporters have come knocking on our doors, asking to do a – what is that thing called – *feature* on you? The rhythm of your body, the intricate footwork, your *abhinaya*, your *nazakat*...Kathak runs in your blood! The courtesans..."

"Stop that about the courtesans!" Naina said sharply. "I love you very much, Bua," she continued in a softer voice, with a smile that briefly filled out her pinched face. "But I only want to focus on my music now. As for dance, I have neither the desire nor the dedication. I feel so tired these days... If I had committed to the show, so much time would have gone in practice. Now at least I can rest a bit, and then..."

"Nonsense! All nonsense! You will never rest!" her aunt exclaimed, beating her forehead dramatically. "Don't I know you? You will find another bunch of girls and start a new music class, you will use the extra money to get some broken part of this haveli repaired, you will buy me shoes and medicines, and nothing for yourself. And then, when the rains come and the pipes start leaking and the roof comes crashing over our head again, you will sit up the whole night with pen and paper, calculating how much more of your blood you need to give, to keep me and this bloodsucking old house alive! *Hey Bhagwan*, if only your father had not squandered all his wealth away, if only he had thought about his family…!"

"Don't criticise Babuji," Naina said, thinking of her father, the gentle man in the worn-out shoes who had always ensured that his family was well-fed, that his sick wife – Naina's mother – had the doctors and expensive medicines she needed, and that Naina got a good education. She remembered the deep lines of fatigue on his face when he returned from work well after sunset, but he would never complain when his wife's groans kept the whole household from sleeping. Instead, he would sit up entire nights to rub hot oil on her painfully swollen body, murmuring words of endearment until she finally fell asleep.

"You will work harder and harder…" Naina's aunt was saying.

"And don't make me sound like a saint, because I'm not," Naina said, her eyes still and deep, far deeper than her twenty-two years. "I do what I do for a purely selfish reason, and that is to try and hold on to the few things I love, the few things I have left in this world. One of them is you, the other is this house."

"I know, I know," her aunt grumbled, spitting some more betel juice and wiping her mouth with the frayed edge of her dupatta. "And it's almost time for your classes. I hope they pay you your salary today, the bloodsucking leeches. Do you want some tea before you go?"

"Yes, I would love some tea, with *laung* and *elaichi*," Naina said, pressing her hand against the dull, familiar throb in her temples.

"Good. Go make some for yourself, and pour out a nice big glass for your *bua*," her aunt said, stretching out her stubby legs on the *charpai* and starting to snore almost immediately, her mountain belly rising and falling like a curse.

✦

Naina walked down the dusty lane, her feet trained to avoid the potholes and open drains spewing garbage. She had lost seven kilos since summer, and her walk was not as brisk as it used to be. Kneading her right temple, she briefly wondered what it might be like to be in bed for an entire day. No household chores to attend to, no classes to teach, no clutter; just to sleep on and on, while the sun rose high, shone through, and sank low at dusk.

The day held no surprises. The same orange sky, smoke-filled, smouldering. The same city of nomads, crowds milling everywhere, elbows and knees. The same blare of traffic, the brittle roads, the buses tilting dangerously around the bends. Even the faces of the men on the buses seemed all the same; their hands touching her here and pinching her there, the bodies pressed hard against hers. Taking after her parents and their old city culture of quiet grace, Naina had never been particularly aggressive. During her college years, however, she would at least try to strike out spiritedly against this man, complain against that one. Time had stamped out even that little ember; now, she was just a woman in a crowded bus who couldn't afford to be late for work.

As the bus tilted and swerved again, she clung on more tightly to the overhead rod with one hand and wiped the small beads of sweat on her upper lip with the other. Through the broken windows, she could see the sleek, expensive cars on the road, the Fords, the Skodas, the beautiful women sitting inside them, expensive clothes, hair stylishly cut, faces perfectly made up. Sometimes their eyes met, across the road and everything else that divided them, and Naina thought—perhaps she is unhappy too.

The music school on Deen Dayal Upadhyay Marg was quite well-known, and Naina was lucky they had hired her as a part-time classical music teacher on the basis of her music certificates and two rounds of auditions. The youngest among a very talented faculty, she felt grateful for the meagre but steady monthly salary she was able to earn. She knew that her job also gave her official credibility, without which it would have been difficult to get the students she now had for private tuitions. In the beginning, the sounds of the tabla and the tanpura, the *sargam*s reverberating off the school's faded walls, used to fill her with an incredible joy, a sense of oneness with the universe. Now, as she walked past those same walls, it was just a job.

✦

It was almost six by the time Naina finished teaching her classes and boarded the *mudrika* for Vasant Vihar. A much longer journey, through congested black roads coiled snakishly around the city and spewing a million venomous tongues of smoke. When she got off the bus an hour later, the last of the sun had dribbled into the horizon and the evening was the colour of pale oatmeal. Coughing to clear her throat, she hailed an autorickshaw. "Bhaiya, D-Block. *Jaldi.*"

It always filled her with dread, this shiny part of Delhi, its wide roads flanked by bungalows, the smooth cars, spotless sidewalks, the crisp smell of money. And the house that still loomed in and out of her dreams: the furtive corners of its garden, that armchair and the jagged shadow it cast over the hallway, the stairs that led to hidden rooms with their lavender bedsheets, convenient, suffocating. But it was just two classes a week, for eight thousand rupees a month plus travel expenses. Sometimes, even an old *zari* sari or a pretty trinket; they had bought her out.

Today, the security guard was looking on with sympathy as she struggled out of the autorickshaw in the stony evening light, her bags, her mirrored dupatta, her long hair all getting in the way. "Varun baba is here. He – the two of them – just arrived," the guard said quietly, in response to her greeting.

So they all knew, didn't they? Ultimately, the furtiveness of gardens, of winding stairways and hidden rooms, of shadows short and long, all come to this: an ungentle, public knowing. Eyes shimmering, Naina lifted her chin proudly. "I see. Will they stay long?"

"*Pata nahi*. They might, they might not. Why don't you go straight up to *bitiya*'s room?"

"I will. Thank you," she replied, turning away and walking quickly down the brick-laid path and into the marbled foyer. But before she could run up the stairs, Mrs. Vadera was waddling out with a great sense of purpose.

"Namaste, Neelima Aunty," Naina said carefully, heart thudding.

"Namaste, Namaste. You are exactly on time," breathed Mrs. Vadera. "Good, good. Before you go up to Vartika's room, you must, must come and see who's here! It's a surprise, a surprise."

Neelima Vadera did not repeat her words for greater effect; no, she was an ineffectual woman and knew it. It had taken Naina a year to understand that Neelima's words were, like her face, a smokescreen, their true intent carefully concealed beneath layers of make-up. She was not vicious.

Only, years of living in the shadows of her husband and her son had made her something of a spectator; she liked a good show.

"We'll get late for Vartika's music lesson, Aunty—"

"You take your work too seriously, too seriously," Neelima said, gripping Naina's arm tightly and dragging her into the living room. "Five or ten minutes won't make a difference. Everyone, see who we have here, see, see!"

There was silence in the room. It must have slipped their minds that Naina would be coming for Vartika's Monday music lesson around that time of evening. To Naina, it seemed so surreal: the vivid red of the couch, the rug with its swirly, deceptive pattern, the cream walls, the pretty people hanging around like framed paintings on a wall...frozen. She wanted to enter again, this time with more poise, not a hair out of place, smiling. *Hello, hello everyone, how nice to see you, and now if you don't mind, I would like to kill you all...*

Ashok Vadera was the first to recover. "Naina, my child," he pronounced with equanimity, drawing on his pipe and blowing out a smooth ring of smoke.

Over time, Naina had learnt the many different shades in his voice. It could be breathy, guttural, like the day when she had bent to dust her sandals, and his eyes had rested on the soft tumble of her breasts. "You're a pretty thing, aren't you," he'd rasped, tucking a stray tendril of hair behind her ear. "Come and join me in the study. To discuss Vartika's progress." When Naina had tonelessly replied that she would rather wait for his wife to return from her club, his eyes had narrowed into slits. Yet a couple of weeks later, when he'd chanced upon Varun tickling Naina in the hallway, his approval of her had been almost fatherly. "That's my boy! And Naina, you come to me if he ever troubles you too much and I'll set him straight," he'd said with a grin, before disappearing into his study. Months later, the same voice, carrying clearly through the flimsy walls, had been authoritative, admonishing. "She's way below our class, Varun. I thought it was a silly flirtation and would be over quickly. But you dragged it on, and now she's following you around like a faithful dog everywhere. End it, before it gets out of hand."

"Namaste Uncle," Naina said mechanically, her eyes on Varun. "Hello, Varun."

"Hi Naina," Varun said easily. "*Kaise ho aap*?" He was leaning against the fireplace, one hand in the pocket of his immaculate trousers, a glass of whiskey in the other. There was a chandelier directly above him, and lights danced in his glass. "Would you like a drink?" he asked, switching to English. "Dad and I are having whiskey, Ma's having sherry and Kats is having a cosmopolitan..."

"You know I don't drink," Naina replied in English. "And I was just telling your mother that we are getting late for Vartika's *riyaaz*, so I think I'll run upstairs. It's getting late, and I have to get back home in time."

"We can always get the driver to drop you home," Varun replied, his eyes holding hers.

"That's very kind of you, but you shouldn't spoil my habits," Naina said, with as much composure as she could muster.

"Come, come, my dear," said Ashok, getting up to put his arm around Naina's shoulders. "You can't be in such a hurry. You and Varun are meeting after so many months; you haven't even congratulated him on his wedding yet."

"I was hurt you didn't attend the ceremony, Naina," Varun said, watching her carefully. "Kats and I had rather hoped you would..."

Naina's eyes were drawn to the lights dancing in his glass, to the frothy amber liquid he swirled round and round for no reason. When she gulped, she could almost taste the whiskey in his glass and on his luscious, lying lips. She wanted to stop being dignified for once, to snatch the glass out of his hand, to be a tongue loosened by alcohol. Her whole body a tongue, magnificent in its fury, lashing out a hundred taunts. Eight thousand rupees, plus travel and trinkets. "I am sorry," she said, looking away. "My aunt was sick, I had to be with her. Congratulations. And congratulations to you too, Karishma."

Karishma was the daughter of Ashok Vadera's long-time business partner. As light-skinned as Naina, but harder, fuller, like the stone carvings in the temples of Khajuraho. Thick-lipped, broad-hipped, high-breasted. A modern-day nymph, in shapely jeans, an off-shoulder blouse, and six-inch wedge heels. "Thanks Naina," she said, with a wave of her manicured hand. "I hope you can join us for dinner. Right, Mamma?"

"Yes, of course, of course," said Neelima, coming forward with arms outstretched. "Naina will join us for dinner, won't you, *beta*? In an hour?"

Nodding, Naina turned to go upstairs. From the stairway, she could hear Karishma's voice, crystal clear. "This Naina, she speaks English quite fluently, and without any accent. Quite impressive. Who could ever imagine?"

Then Neelima. "She studied in a good English-medium school. College diploma too. They don't have much money, but I believe the father made sure she got a good education."

Karishma again. "And she's been moving in the right circles. Her clothes may be tacky, but she's pretty. With a little polish, she could do quite well, don't you think, Varun? I feel bad for her."

"So take her under your wing, teach her some style and set her up with a nice guy." A laugh. "Wotsay, Dad?"

"You all can be so mean, so mean." Neelima, breathless.

"Why? We're a modern family, we take everything in our stride. Ex-girlfriends and wives live in happy harmony. What's so mean about that, motherhood?" Varun's laughter again.

To Naina, leaning weakly against the bannisters, his laugh sounded…familiar. Its rumble, its upturned edges, its cocooning swell. Oh, yes. A few months ago, Karishma had had some trouble with the police. She'd been driving home after a late night party, and had failed the breath test. Her father, then in London for a business meeting, had called to ask for Ashok Vadera's help; Ashok, in turn, had asked his son to drive across and see what the matter was. "They are family friends, and her father says she had a little wine, that's all," he'd yelled from downstairs. "She says the cops are just trying to make money. Look here, we've got to take a stand."

Squeezed against the utilities closet, with his hands splayed warmly over Naina's stomach, Varun had sighed in exasperation. "The only stand I am willing to take for that woman is a one-night stand. Seriously, have you seen that body?" Tickling Naina's breast with the corner of a folded, lavender-scented bed sheet, he'd laughed. A slow, deep, delicious laugh, just like this one.

Truths and Troubles

"Epistemology. A theory of knowledge," Megan intoned. "But what do we mean by knowledge? How do we know? How do we settle competing truth claims? And what, for that matter, *is* truth?"

Two dozen heads, black, brown, blonde, ash-grey, some looking out of the window and chewing gum, others nodding solemnly, pens in hand. The overhead projector beaming a blue ray of light onto the hanging screen; dancing images of Plato, Aristotle, Marx, Sartre, Freud, Derrida. The intermittent gurgles of the water cooler outside. And a branch of that burning tree, poking, elbow-like, against the corner window.

"Foundationalists believe there is an absolute ground for truth. For the rationalist Plato, this foundation was reason; for the empiricist Aristotle, it was the senses, and systematic scientific enquiry. Can anyone tell us the names of some modern foundationalists?"

A hand shot up. Carly. The girl was from a blue-collar neighbourhood nearby, Megan remembered, and easily one of the best students in the class. "Rene Descartes," she said. "He was rationalist too, right? Like Plato? And Francis Bacon was an empiricist, the father of modern science."

"Excellent," Megan said, making a mental note to speak to her afterwards about applying for the Rhodes scholarship. She remembered the day Carly had first entered class: pierced eyebrows, ripped jeans, tattoos, somehow determined not to succeed.

"So antifoundationalism emerged in response to the foundationalist claim of 'true' knowledge as certain and absolute. Some antifoundationalist names, anyone?"

This time it was the Indian boy, the second generation immigrant. "Thomas Hobbes, David Hume. In *Leviathan,* Hobbes argued that there is no essential relation between... er...words and things."

"Correct. So what was his solution to the complex issues of language and meaning, and the fallibility of knowledge?"

"Wasn't it a political solution?" he replied, after some thought. "Sovereignty and the social contract?"

"Excellent! In our next class, we shall discuss how, differences aside, all these frameworks were profoundly androcentric. Then we shall go on to see how feminist theories give us alternative frameworks through which to interpret knowledge and understand the question of truth. But before we end today's class, can anyone tell us what is androcentrism?"

"Privileging the masculine point of view. A sophisticated word to describe fucking patriarchy," spat out a student from the back row without bothering to raise her hand, angry red curls tumbling over a pixie face. She'd recently come out of the closet, and was, by her own description, the last of the radicals. "Yes, I have sex with women and have no plans of stopping," she'd said to a shell-shocked class early on in the term.

Megan was quite fond of the teenager and her brusque ways. "Okay," she said with a grin, distributing the handouts she had prepared earlier. "So this has a list of next week's presentations. Be sure to read the articles carefully. And like I always say, the course material means nothing if we only use it to write term papers. Our relationship with our books must be more organic; we must grow with, critique, adapt and transform the material, make it more meaningful for our lives. That's what I want you to do with the articles for next week. Go beyond the dense language and try to grasp the core, okay? See you Monday. Have a great weekend."

When the class had emptied out, leaving behind a jumble of chairs, crumpled paper and indistinct, week-old smells, Megan glanced back to see Segun slumped in his chair as usual. Catching her eye, he began to shuffle to his feet, an awkward boy-man. As the first few weeks of term had gone by, Megan had watched him slide lower and lower in his seat. Sometimes, in the middle of a lecture, she would see his faded eyes fix on the chalkboard, trying to comprehend; at other times, she imagined the light flicker in those eyes as they darted towards the wall-clock, waiting for his incarceration to end. In her new city, melancholy was nothing new. But this was different; she could see something in him was slowly dying.

"Segun. I need to speak with you," she said briskly, making a quick decision. "You do know you are in danger of failing this course, don't you? Missing classes, not participating in class discussions. I haven't even seen a draft of your essay. The university requires professors to send warnings to students in writing, but I thought I would have a little – how shall I put it – informal chat with you instead."

The boy looked first at her, then at the windows, and through them, the expanse of sky. He was well over six feet tall and muscular, but in that moment he was a child, wandering, lost. Megan felt a surge of affection. "You are from Nigeria, aren't you?" she asked, her voice gentler. He nodded.

"I have a Nigerian connection too," Megan continued. "Well, sort of. Never been there myself, but my parents lived there for a year. My father speaks very fondly of Nigeria."

Segun looked at her curiously. "In Abuja?"

"No. Lagos. On Victoria Island, I believe. He still makes *suya*, you know, those grilled chicken bits in some sort of powdered batter – tahini, I think it is –"

"*Suya*," Segun said, remembering. "Victoria Island, dat too cost. The Island don big shops…big houses…and clubs."

"Yes, my father does mention a local club he used to go to, and the friends he made there. So what's the best thing you liked about Nigeria?"

He bit his lip. "Pipo in Nigeria, dem togetha. Play, laugh, fight…but always togetha, like brodas. In Amerika, dem on dia own. Time wey I small, we – my Baba, his broda and me – went to di bay by awa speedboat. Afta we land in Amerika, it is my moda only, and her leg no der stay in one place. I miss my Baba."

"Hmm. I can understand you're unhappy," Megan said. "Sometimes the present makes us unhappy, and it is not something to be ashamed of. What is important is that we figure out how to create a better future. Agree?"

When he nodded, she drew out her pen and writing pad. "Three things," she said, jotting down points. "First, I need you to start attending class regularly. Second, I need you to participate in class—no, don't look scared. You can just say one or two things, even stuff in the readings you didn't understand, so we can use your inputs to get a discussion going. Get it? And third, I will set aside two hours for you every week, just before my regular office hours, so I can go over the week's readings with you."

"Uh. Special coaching?"

"Well, you could say that."

"And you der charge me moni for this, yes?"

Megan rubbed her palms together and laughed delightedly. "Heck no! I am just trying to help you do well at school, so you can get a nice job when you graduate and build a good life for yourself here in this country."

"Okay. You are from Nigeria."

"No, like I said, I've never been, but my father -"

"No. You are from Nigeria," he said, a slight tremor in his lower lip. "My own don betta. You help me."

At an uncharacteristic loss for words, Megan patted him on the back. "So, I want to see a more focused, hard-working Segun from next week. Promise?

He nodded. "But what...about classes I...miss already?" he asked, trying to switch over from pidgin English with effort. "I will not fail? Maybe you...only minus one grade, yes?"

"Hmm, let's see. How about we just overlook your past absences? In fact, tell you what, I won't even deduct a grade, but only as long as you start doing the things I have just outlined for you. In which case, I will give you your final grade based on your performance next week onwards. Now, go back to your dorm, grab some dinner, get some sleep. We got a lot of work to do from next week."

✦

Megan came out of the classroom and stood in the foyer of Henderson Hall. A few crossings away, the city waited: a living, snarling beast. Shutters down at six, commuters on their way home by the New Jersey Transit, business districts emptying the last of their litter onto the sidewalks. A few hours of unquiet after that; rows of high-rise offices staring down glassily over Broad and Market Streets, parking lots, subway stations, numb. And then, as night began to fall, snarls everywhere, boots with serrated edges, trash-cans being kicked about in metallic cacophony. Guns would find – and just as often, miss – their mark; homeless bodies huddled by the dumpsters would live and die. At night, the streets of Newark were godless and unforgiving, and the white powders that switched palms blew up a smoke so thick and giddy it drowned out the stars.

At least the university was safe. While daylight robberies and hate crimes were not unheard of even on campus, the crime-alerts beeped by the police department keeping everyone on an endless edge, the buildings on College Boulevard bore very little resemblance to the grim, bullet-ridden ones in the inner city. On campus, within the comforting grid of desks and chalkboards and libraries and cafeterias, there was beauty, knowledge, and the promise of a redgold tree. Ever since her move to Newark, this was her little grid of normalcy, a place to talk of tomorrow.

She waited for the last lot of students to straggle past with their books, laptops, Coke cans, shoulder thumps, laughter. Then, taking off her chunky wedges and slipping them into her bag, she pulled out her rubber flip-flops and slid into them with a groan. Twenty years ago, on a random trip to the beach, she and her father had solemnly agreed that flip-flops were the world's best*est* invention *ever*. Dear Dad. She couldn't wait to see him this weekend.

✦

The walk would take exactly twenty minutes, not allowing for mishaps. She walked out through the revolving door, and into the fading orange light of evening.

There was no traffic signal just outside the building. In all of campus, this was one magic spot; each time you wanted to cross over, the cars somehow picked up on your intention and, howsoever precariously, stopped. There had never been an accident. Megan smiled apologetically when the cars halted, a truck missing her flowing skirt by inches. A tattooed man at the wheel grinned back with enthusiasm, his hand thumping a beat on the dashboard so loud it could probably be heard all the way down to Connecticut. Ignoring him, Megan continued to walk in the evening half-light, turning the corner around the Washington Street subway. *Karim Street. Karim Street.* The thought that had been floating inside her through the day, fragile, threadlike, was now weaving itself into a spider's web.

There was very little doubt in her mind as to the inherent truth of the letter. A little girl's curly-haired question: *How come you and Dad are so pale and I darker?* Hell, now that she thought about it, there weren't even any pictures of her mother's pregnancy; just of her holding a baby swaddled in white. Yet, three years later, there was an entire album for her brother Jeff: Mother, weary-eyed, big-bellied, and Dad, dancing in a clown's cap, happy.

Embedded bits of her childhood were dislodging themselves, hurtling out. *What is truth, and how do we know?* The question she was fond of posing to her class had now twisted itself around her in a tight band. And her heart's response, one that would have fetched her students a failing grade: sometimes, truth just *is*. Sometimes we just know.

Instead of turning left at the Broad Street intersection for home, she walked rapidly down Market Street, leaving one crossing, two, three, four, and there it was: the bright green neon light that said *Karim's*.

On her first weekend in Newark, when she hadn't yet discovered the grid of restaurants, grocery stores and buzzing fish markets in the nearby Portuguese neighbourhood called the Ironbound, Kevin, who was visiting, had asked his GPS for directions to the nearest restaurant. The starchy female voice on the system had directed them here, to this marketplace grill, with its neon lights and, somewhat incongruously, a window poster of a litter of cats.

"I'll go grab us some food. You sit in the car and keep your windows rolled up," Kevin had said urgently.

"Don't be ridiculous!" She'd snapped. "What am I, six?"

Kevin had thrown back his head and laughed. "Never let a guy take care of you, will you? Fine, come on out. Just be careful with your pocketbook—no, don't leave it in the car. And wait, lemme roll up the windows."

"Whatever." She'd sat in the car, watching Kevin ward off an unshaved man in a threadbare jersey limping up to ask for money. The man was thin, so thin his cheeks had disappeared into a blue hollow and his hip bone stuck out. She'd wished Kevin would give the man a couple of bucks, but Kevin, as it turned out, had had a better plan; emerging a few minutes later with boxes of food in his hand, he'd given the man a box.

"Boy, that was quick," Megan had said, when he got into the car. "I am *starving*. And hey, it was nice of you to buy that man his dinner."

"Yeah. So I have shish kebabs, with fries. Seedy joint, but I can tell you that it smells divine in there," he'd said with an appreciative sniff. "I would not recommend walking down here by yourself late at night though. No, I'm serious. There's a menu inside one of the boxes; just order delivery if you have to."

It was then that Megan had seen her: a woman in a miniskirt, purple printed tights, and a blouse entirely too skimpy to contain the high spill of her breasts. A goddess of the night, with glossy, almost sculpted features, bright red lipstick and a mole on the chin.

Kevin had coughed. "Some area you've moved into, Meg. All we need is some drug peddlers and a shooting spree to make it completely homey."

"Shut up, dickhead. There are hookers in New York too. I once saw one around Tenth Avenue, and once in Brooklyn. Criminalisation of prostitution is so *medieval* anyway. The state posturing as a custodian of public morality, telling us to go to church and not the whorehouse! Where *is* our modernity? It's her body, her choice."

"You shut up now. Let's get the hell outta here, before there's any more action," Kevin had replied tersely, reversing the car.

Pulling a face at him, Megan had craned her neck to get one last glimpse of the cinched waist, the shapely buttocks and two long, long legs flashing under the neon lights. "She's beautiful," Megan had whispered.

✦

The memory of that evening, so light and fresh, now stale. Is this the Karim Street of the unnamed writer's poison pen, she wondered uneasily. And what in hell's name could possibly be *my* connection to it? Is that why fate brought me to this city?

Megan breathed deeply, telling herself to stop being dramatic. Since when had she believed in fate? And what was her problem really—that she was not her parents' daughter? Or that she came from a family of prostitutes? So *what*? Her body her choice. Hadn't those been her own words?

She looked around, but it probably wasn't night enough for the girl with the sashaying hips and the painted mole. The neon light was blinking furiously, and a homeless man huddled next to the cat-litter poster laughed. This is all getting a bit much, Megan suddenly thought. There must be a dozen shish kebab places called Karim's on east coast alone, and the official Karim streets in the world must number hundreds.

She had to be *crazy* to be standing here, crazy to even be thinking about that ridiculous letter!

Dismissing the idea of buying dinner, Megan turned and started walking away quickly, quickly past the subway and the linen store, her long strides eating up the breathless half-mile till she finally entered Rose Lane. Some of these side streets could be quite dodgy at night; for now, there was still a shade of light, sallow, intermittent, saving her from nameless crimes while she groped about in her purse for the keys and let herself in.

The lobby, familiar, a lover's embrace. She remembered when she'd first come to look at these apartments, and had been struck by all the art hanging on the walls, very tasteful, the rushes in the urns, the elevators gleaming, the carpets well-worn yet elegant. It was only after she'd signed the lease and stepped out of the building that she noticed the garbage dump—black plastic bags, one burst open, spewing rags and rotten eggs. Calculating that the dump would be just beneath the second-floor window of her apartment, she'd rushed back in, wanting to cancel the lease, but the manager was nowhere to be found. She'd never thought of herself as particularly squeamish, but she'd smelt the trash for days afterwards, during her last weekend in Princeton, in her sleep, among her scented bed sheets. And felt guilty, so guilty. Privilege, that textbook word, suddenly real...

The elevator doors slid open, and a couple stepped out. He was well-dressed and she laughed gaily on his arm. For the second time that day, Megan was reminded of William, of the elegant dinners they would go for, how she would dab on his favourite perfume and check her profile in the mirror a dozen times, how he hated to be kept waiting. Perhaps anonymous letters are supposed to bring back memories of all the catastrophes that have ever befallen you, she grimaced, walking out of the elevator and into her apartment.

Flicking on the lights, she sank tiredly into her new sofa. She and the apartment didn't belong together just yet, even though she padded about early each morning in her nightdress, much before the sun was up, trying to learn all the crooks and crevices. Only the bathroom felt homely, her fluffy white bathrobe hanging from the hook behind the door, the magazine rack filled with old issues of *Homes and Gardens*, the towels minty fresh, the shower curtains so pretty.

Ah, those shower curtains. They reminded her of her first evening in Newark, right after she'd moved in. She'd gone across to the dollar store to buy the curtains, a pattern of pink roses and ferns, and she'd hummed an old tune. Deciding to explore the city afterwards, she was on her way back home an hour or so later when she was followed. A loose-limbed man in his late twenties, early thirties at the most. "You're pretty," he'd growled every few minutes. It was dark, the side street empty and unending. She'd started walking faster. He'd looked almost apologetic, but had continued to follow her anyway. Not the swaggering stroll of the street lout or the hardened march of the criminal; rather, the walk of the addict, numbed out of his senses, wanting to do something, anything, just to feel alive.

Summoning her street smarts, she'd slipped around the corner of a building and dialled 911. When she'd finished narrating her experience, the voice on the other end had drily enquired whether the man had done anything to her. "What do you mean, *done* anything to me?" she'd asked hotly. "He's following me! Can't you send some backup?"

Not in Newark they couldn't. In Newark, there were strong-arm robberies and drug dealings even as they were speaking, and a petty stalker didn't amount to much. "Sorry we cannot do anything at this point, but please call back if there is any evidence of threatening behaviour. In the meantime, please continue to be aware of your surroundings. Do not display money or electronic equipment. Seek the safety of crowds. Keep to the main roads, and avoid dimly-lit spaces."

Swearing under her breath, she'd walked out of the corner and onto the street again. The man was loping towards her. She'd returned the cellphone to her bag and balled her right fist. She may not have completed that karate class in high school, but she wasn't some cowering little thing who couldn't put up a fight if she had to. He was barely ten inches away from her. She'd hardened her eyes and looked at him squarely. "Excuse me, miss, would you have five bucks to spare?" He'd asked her then, flashing a broken-toothed smile.

The same guilt, only a scream this time instead of a whimper. "Yes, yes," she'd said, unzipping her pocketbook.

"I teach my students to challenge stereotypes, and look at me," she'd remarked to an older woman checking her mail in the lobby, once she was back inside her building. "There was this guy following me…I thought he was going to attack me, but he really just wanted a couple of bucks. All these crazy stories about crime around here...mostly bullshit, right?"

The woman had looked at her wryly. "Nothing crazy there. Poverty and hunger breed crime. The couple on the fourth floor had their car broken into this week. And Doc James on the fifth is still nursing a broken jaw…two men followed him back from the train station to snatch his laptop. There's so much drugs on these streets it's insane. Anyway, cops do patrol this area; you'll hear shots being fired sometimes in the night. Haven't heard of rape, but I guess you gotta be careful."

That first night, Megan had stayed awake while the wind howled the lids off the trashcans directly below her window.

Every once in a while, there was a hollow cough followed by the striking of a matchstick. From behind her silk drape, she'd seen the nubs of fire whizzing through the thick blue night. But when she'd parted the curtains to try and make out the moving shapes in the dark, she'd seen squares and cylinders, men and trashcans, and couldn't tell which was which.

Over the next few days, the moving shapes in the city had become people again, homeless, who lived without tax or insurance, stocked up on eighty-nine cent cans of rice and beans, and slept amid trashcans in the night when the city shelters were full. Once Megan had gone down to the pharmacy along the main road and was paying for her Tylenol and Pepsid when the man in front of her started throwing up on the floor. Some of his vomit had splashed onto Megan's boots. Everyone in the pharmacy had gone about their daily business without a second look. On her way back home, she'd stopped at the garbage dump to shrug off her boots.

That night she'd called Kevin to tell him about the incidents of that week. "I'm not going to pretend it isn't hard. The hardest part is being confronted by my…my own self. You know? But I signed up for this, and I'm going to see it through. I'm not giving up," she'd said quietly, when he'd asked if she wanted to come back to Princeton. "And I love the kids."

He'd understood. Gently reminding her to put away her favourite diamond brooch and not wear it on the streets, he'd promised he would drive up to see her that weekend. After he hung up, she'd curled up into a ball and gone to sleep on the couch. Waking up in the morning, she'd taken a cold shower and decided to embrace her new life in earnest. Two months later, things had become a lot less hard.

That is, until earlier this morning. Damn that letter.

✦

Slipping out of the bath and into her bathrobe, she turned up the radio. Norah Jones was huskily crooning '*Baby I see you for who you are; one time apple queen, one time tramp,*' and Megan found herself smiling. Grabbing a can of Coke from the fridge, she dialled a familiar number.

He always smiled when he heard the phone ring, even before he knew who it was, the corners of his eyes crinkling in the anticipation that it might be some forgotten friend from far away. "Hullo? Meg?"

"Hey Dad."

"I was just thinking of you! How's it going?"

Awesome. I learned that you and Mother are not my real parents. Which is something I've suspected for a while, so no worries. "Long day, Dad."

"So what are you doing calling your father? Put on a dress, dab on some lipstick and go to the city for cocktails and dinner with some nice guy. Caviar, Vivaldi in the background, pop open a bottle of champagne maybe..."

She was laughing now. "Yeah, right. And the guy in question is, of course, Kevin?"

"Well. He could be."

"No, he couldn't. I don't know if you will ever get it, but he's my *best friend*, for God's sake. We've never felt romantically for each other!"

"Your mother and I were best friends too. That's the most important thing. Increasingly so, as the sexual begins to take a backseat."

"Oh, never mind."

"Your mother would say that too, you know? In exactly that tone! 'Never mind Stan,' she'd go, whenever I got too insistent. Your mother—"

Megan exhaled. "Let's not talk about her, please? Not today."

There was a long silence on the other end. Then her father cleared his throat. "All right. Tell me about your day. How was it?"

"The usual," Megan lied. *Adoption is no big deal. Why couldn't you just tell me?* "Can't wait to see you tomorrow."

"If you take the dinky, I'll pick you up at Princeton. Maybe we could have lunch before driving back home? There's this new place that's just opened on Nassau Street –"

"Dad, do you think we could drive home directly? And cook lunch together, like we used to? Lay about, listen to some music, look at some family albums maybe?"

"Hmm. Is everything alright, Meg?"

I think I'm being blackmailed by a stranger. "Yup. Just want to feel at home again."

"No problem. We can do whatever you want. It'll be good for me to get some rest too. My rheumatism has been acting up and—"

"Hell. Why didn't you tell me? Did you speak to Joe? Are you taking your meds? Eating properly?"

"Yes, yes. Don't worry, Joe will drop by next week. He won't hear of my finding another doctor in Pennington. It's just a fifteen-minute drive for him from Princeton, he says."

"I don't know why Jeff and Angela can't come look you up. They're just a fifteen-minute drive away too! "

"Megan, I'm all right, really. And I will feel so much better once you are here. Besides, I am growing old, you know. Your dad's growing old, and these aches and pains are here to stay."

"Nonsense. You're not old. You look better than guys half your age! Listen, let's do lunch at home like I said. Afterwards, if you feel like it, we can go out for dinner to some place close by. The pizza place you mentioned the other day, maybe?"

"Sounds good."

"Okay then, I'll see you at eleven at the station. Good night."

"Good night, sweetheart."

She could see him so clearly, silhouetted against a sepia sky. Faded pair of jeans and light woollen jersey, black-rimmed glasses, comfortable slippers. Silver-haired but still handsome, a glass of chardonnay in one hand and a book in the other. He loved sunrises, sunsets, liked how the changing light made everything mellow in the woods. "Nature never lies," he would always say.

But what about you, Dad, Megan murmured. What about you?

The Album

The Trenton train on the north-east corridor whizzed across New Jersey, taking Megan on her weekend visit to Princeton. Visit. A funny word, for a city that ran in your blood. And yet, forty-five minutes later, when she got off at Princeton Junction and walked towards the picturesque little train that was locally referred to as the dinky, the smell of another city fresh on her skin, that's really what it seemed like—a visit, to an old lover perhaps, while the new one fumed and waited.

Sitting on the dinky for the last ten minutes of her journey into Princeton, everything seemed easy. She imagined her father, his arm around her shoulder, his eyes deeply sympathetic. "Yes, you're adopted, and so sorry I didn't tell you this earlier. Your mother's health, the background of your real family...didn't know how you would react. But you're *my* daughter, and don't you ever forget that."

It was that simple, she thought with a smile, getting off the dinky and walking up to the street, her step light. So light it lifted her entirely out of the present, and again, into the cloudy memory of an older angst. Especially when she saw the McCarter Theater across the street. The memory of that afternoon, still so vivid, when she'd worn a new dress, tucked a flower in her hair and smiled at strangers...William had arrived an hour late, without an excuse, and they'd driven off to look at houses for him. He'd zeroed in on a yellow-bricked mansion with wrought-iron gates. Sunlight bounced off the walls of the house, snatches of it caught in the glass windows. "I *love* it! When you're gone for your conferences, I'll come and live here," she'd said, hopping out of the car barefoot.

"Put your sandals on. The estate agent will be here anytime," he'd said tersely, but she'd whooped into his arms, smothering him with kisses. He'd kissed her back, and she'd felt him hot against her skin, and slipped her hand inside his shirt, and her lips had followed, and he'd groaned and she'd wanted him there, right there...

She was probably missing the sex, she thought viciously. There could be absolutely *no* other reason – no, not even the letter – why she would think of him thrice in one week. Whatever it was, she needed to stop it. *Now.*

Megan put on her sunglasses and scanned the street. There it was, her father's convertible turning the corner. When the stylish green Lotus slid to a stop inches away from her, all unpleasant thoughts vanished. "Hey Dad! Good to see you!"

Stanley Adams stepped out of his car, arms outstretched. "Good to see you too, Meg. Hop right in."

The drive from Princeton station to Pennington was enchanting: country roads, a robin blue sky, woodlands on either side, pine and cedar, and lakes circled by geese in the hundreds, their white wings flapping in tandem.

As the grey stone house sequestered by rows of trees came into view, Megan turned to her father. "I can see why you chose Acres Drive instead of Princeton, or even downtown Pennington. It really is beautiful, Dad. So much land, and such *spectacular* views. The only other time I was here, I must have been too preoccupied to notice."

"Yes, exactly the kind of house I wanted," Stanley replied. He would have relocated to the suburbs years ago if the Princeton house hadn't been so convenient for his children while they were still at grad school. Jeff had moved out long back, so after Megan shifted to Newark, he'd figured he could finally move too.

Megan squeezed her father's hand. "There's so much silence here, no cars honking or students yelling out to each other from across the street! Just the chirping of birds."

"Speaking of which, you should see my new birdhouse," he said, operating the garage door with a remote. "We get some beautiful birds here—woodpeckers, cardinals, bluejays."

"Look, isn't that a cardinal?" Megan asked, pointing to a brilliantly red bird settling on a droopy branch just above the garage.

Her father nodded, expertly manoeuvring the car. "Let me take your things. I'll pour you a glass of wine, and then let's get cracking on the chicken."

Later, over a lunch of roast chicken, rosemary potatoes and glasses of chilled chardonnay, Stanley turned to his daughter. "What happened about the problem with the student? The one who used to disrupt class?"

"Oh, *that* one," Megan said with a sigh. "I finally told her off. In class. I guess I could have called her to my office, but it was one of those rare cases when I just wasn't comfortable meeting her privately."

"Has her behaviour improved since?"

"She wasn't in class last week," Megan replied, taking a sip of the wine. "Let's see how things are over the next few weeks. I may have to recommend counselling."

Her father nodded. "Sounds like a good solution. You can't handle everything yourself. Try talking to the department head?"

"I think the culture of my university is that they expect faculty to handle stuff themselves. Maybe that's every university nowadays. Who knows. It's all a learning experience for me anyway. Listen, let's talk about something else, please." *Like how I'm adopted.*

"Sure. As for professional challenges, you know I'm here for you whenever you want to talk."

Of course you're there for me, you've always been. I don't care what some stupid anonymous letter says. You're my dad, my one and only. "Thanks, Dad. So how are Jeff and Angela?"

"The last time I saw them was when they were here for dinner. Jeff helped me bring some wood in, and we got a pretty nice fire going. The fireplaces are awesome, have you noticed?"

"Yup. But listen, that dinner was right after you moved in, wasn't it? It's been months! You haven't heard from Jeff since?"

Pouring another glass of wine for himself, Stanley shook his head. "You know Jeff. He wasn't very talkative even when he was here for dinner. Angela made up for it though. She got me some embroidered napkins and a nice bottle of Riesling for a housewarming present. She seemed really taken with the house."

"I may have forgotten to mention it to you, but she called me in Newark the week after I'd moved."

"That's nice of her. I can see she's trying to do her best. Quite a change..."

"Hardly. I happened to mention that I try to avoid going out too late at night in Newark, so she called me supercilious. And a ton of other names."

"Really?"

"Yes. She was like, well, it's ridiculous to aspire to grand ideals, but then to hole oneself up in one's apartment and feel scared. I guess she thinks it's... hypocrisy. Not that I necessarily blame her. Sometimes it feels like hypocrisy to me too. Or inconsistency, at the very least."

"Well, but you *are* a single woman living in a high-crime area," Stanley responded drily, forking a potato. "Angela lives in a million-dollar house in a very posh part of Princeton, remember? No wonder they call us limousine liberals. Doesn't your decision of going to live in Newark mean anything to her?"

"Well, she sounded a bit condescending about it. Maybe she feels I couldn't do better. As in, I don't think she necessarily sees it as idealism. To her, it may just be empty posturing, you know. To mask professional incompetence."

"Huh. Well, I think there's a silver lining to all this stuff," Stanley said, his eyes twinkling. "Maybe it will make you want to move back to Princeton and apply for positions around here. Meg, I miss you. This house brings me so much joy, but it's too large for one person and at the end of the day, I'm on my own. Just memories everywhere, your mother dead, all the people gone..."

"Stop, Dad," Megan said, grinning. "Sometimes you can really get maudlin."

"I know. I wouldn't have thought I had it in me," Stanley replied with a smile. "Age mellows you, makes you want to hold on."

"Come on, it's not like I've moved to a different country," Megan countered. "And the convenience of walking distance to grad school aside, I must have been pretty much the only white girl to not have moved out of home until *thirty*!" Seeing her father look wistful, she stretched her hand across the table to lace her fingers with his. "I miss you too, Dad. Remember the time when I decided you were to be my best friend?"

"Ha! I do. You were all of six, and you wore your brother's baseball cap and some paint on your nose, and marched up to me and announced that I was indeed worthy of the position. You called me Stan – you said, 'Stan, I've given the matter some thought, and I think you can be my best friend from here on' – and your mother almost fainted!"

"I *know*! I think I called you Stan because that's what Mother used to call you..."

"...and when your mother tried to correct you, you stood your ground. 'I want us to be a family of equals', you said. It was hysterical."

Megan threw back her head and laughed. "Oddly enough, I seem to remember that conversation. I remember Mother going off into peals of laughter...I don't think I have any other memory of her laughing quite so hard. She was very serious, wasn't she? And sometimes very...startled, yes, that's the word, startled. Never cheerful, or brisk, or given to laughter. She wasn't like you."

"No, she wasn't," Stanley said, his eyes translucent, filled with pain. "Megan, I'm sorry your memories of her are so difficult. I do remember her laughing. Quite often, in fact."

"Really?"

"Yes. When we were newly married. But then I got busy with my duties as a diplomat.... Slowly, that started getting to your mother. Her early childhood experiences had made her emotionally vulnerable anyway, and I can't imagine the huge age difference between us helped any. The way I think about it is that, as I started easing up, she began to...to shut down."

"Dad, I'm sorry my memories of Mother are so cold," Megan said softly. "I know you loved her. I get that my unwillingness to talk about her, or to do so with such indifference causes you pain, I totally get that. But you have to understand that I didn't know her the way you did. I remember her as distant, too lost in her own world to care..."

"You were only eight when she died," Stanley murmured.

"Yes, I was. And Jeff was five, practically a baby. But the point is that even before she died, as well as for all the years later, you—you were my only parent. Hell, I don't even have a mom-voice in my head the way normal people do! Can you please try to understand that?"

Stanley nodded. "And yet you're so like your mother," he said gruffly. "I don't mean her anxiety or her depression, but in so many other ways. You don't know it, but you are."

Words that would only have aroused a mild sort of curiosity at another time now made her heart skip a beat. "I have to ask you something, Dad," she said carefully. "Does the name Karim Street ring a bell?"

Stanley blinked. "What?... Karim Street? Karim Street. No, I don't know that it does. Why, what is it?"

"Just something that came up in the context of your travels. I thought you might remember."

"In the context of my travels? No. No, I don't. Sounds like a Middle Eastern name, and I haven't been to the Middle East. Except that it does sound strangely familiar too. Karim Street." Stanley screwed his eyes in concentration.

"Maybe something to do with...Mother? I think it was scribbled in one of her books, but I can't remember."

Stanley's eyes flew open. "In one of your mother's books? One of the ones in the library, you mean?" He was staring at Megan intently, and she suddenly felt uncomfortable.

"Never mind, it's silly, probably doesn't mean anything at all," she said, looking away. "Listen, all the activities of the morning must have tired you out. Why don't you go grab yourself a nice siesta while I read in my room?"

"It's an idea. I do tire easily these days," Stanley said, giving his daughter a peck on the cheek.

✦

Megan sprinted up the stairs. The windows in her bedroom were open, a delicious scent of pine wafting in from the dozens of pine trees on the property. She smiled to see the bowl of flowers her father had thoughtfully arranged on her bedside table, the ornate lampstand, the framed photographs and paintings on the walls, the bookshelves and the wicker chairs, and presiding over it all, Empress, her giant-size soft toy pig.

Empress had been a Christmas gift from her father when she was around twelve. "Here we come, the killers of pigs," she and Jeff would growl ominously, jumping on the bed, brandishing their make-believe swords and going after Empress with blood-curdling fury. But at the end of it, the all-forgiving Empress would be back on her shelf, benignly awaiting the next attack. Megan had donated all her stuffed animals to a local charity when she'd graduated high school, but she'd never had the heart to give this one away. "Oh, Empress, I missed you," she said now, hugging its misshapen middle and smiling.

She had just settled into her armchair with a book when there was a knock on the door. "Megan, are you up?"

"Dad? Wassup? I thought you were taking a nap."

The door opened a crack, and her father stuck his neck in. "My memory is not what it used to be, sweetheart, but I think I heard the name Karim Street when your mother and I were in India."

"In *India*?" Megan asked excitedly, jumping to her feet. "Are you quite sure?"

"Well, now, here's the thing," Stanley said, coming into the room. "It's hard to be sure...I mean, it was many years ago, and there must be so many Karim Streets in the world. But there was something about the way you said it...brought back some kind of an association."

"What association? It might be helpful if you could remember, Dad."

"Well, it would be helpful if *you* could remember which book," Stanley replied. "If it's just one of your mother's random scribbles somewhere, you should know we have at least a hundred of her books, and a million of those scribbles! And when did you come across it anyway? Must have been sometime in Princeton. Funny how you never mentioned it up until now."

"I know. It suddenly popped up in my memory, if that makes sense," Megan said, not looking into her father's eyes. "But listen, what made you think it might be India?"

"We were living in New Delhi, but your mother used to go exploring the older parts of the city on her own," said Stanley, remembering. "I think she mentioned the name of that street around then, but I really don't remember too much more. Wait, let me get something for you."

Fifteen minutes later, Stanley returned to Megan's room with his India album. Sitting on her bed, he turned the pages one by one, smiling fondly at the sepia photographs, faded a little over the years yet still very much alive. There she was, his wife and Megan's mother. Sequinned skirt, earrings dangling all the way down to her bare shoulders, eyes heavy with gold shadow. In one photograph, her right arm was looped around the trunk of a tree, its gnarled roots falling all about her while she laughed.

"Wow, look at that tree!" Megan exclaimed. She'd seen most of her parents' travel albums but couldn't quite remember this one.

"That's a banyan, the national tree of India. The aerial roots you see, they grow into thick trunks so that even if the original support tree dies, these other trunks will live on for hundreds of years."

"Fascinating. And such a lovely picture," Megan said, looking more closely. "Mother looks so scandalously exotic!"

Stanley smiled. "You look like her. The resemblance is uncanny."

I don't, and you know it. Why are you doing this, Dad? "Well, at least you were right about her laughing more often. She looks really happy here."

"Yes, doesn't she? Funny as it may sound, I think India was the first place she genuinely felt at home. When we came away, she was heartbroken. In some ways, she never really got over that."

"Why, did she make a lot of friends there?"

Stanley closed his eyes and put his palm on his chest, breathing deeply. When Megan turned his face up to hers, worry in her eyes, he smiled feebly. "I'm fine...I just miss her."

"I know," Megan said softly, placing her hand over his.

"Well, I wouldn't say she made a lot of friends there. Just some *rickshaw-wallah*s and tour guides, their families sometimes. She always managed to avoid the diplomatic circuit, got mysterious headaches right before we had some formal event at the embassy. Your mother's – how should I put it – *inner life* was very fertile. She didn't need people; her relationships were more with cities, and spaces. She'd walk around by herself, hunting for bargains in little nooks, drinking tea out of earthen cups..."

"That sounds so different from the flat memories I have," Megan said, shaking her head in wonder. "Well, you know what? Maybe, instead of that trip to the south of France we keep talking about, we could take a trip to India. What about this winter?"

Stanley looked at his daughter incredulously. "A trip to *India*? What's come over you? You've never been interested in your mother for two decades, yet today you are full of questions about her! You say you found the mention of some street in one of her books, yet can't remember where or what it was. And now you want to go to India? What's going on?"

"Calm down, Dad. Why are you getting so agitated? It's not good for your blood pressure. Going to India was just a thought, and only because we keep talking about a holiday."

Stanley looked at his daughter for a long time. "Is there something you are not telling me, kid?"

For the hundredth time, she wanted to ask him the truth outright; and for the hundredth time, something in her held back. Perhaps her father's tired eyes, or the thought that it was all a big mistake, or the need to buy a little more time in case it wasn't. And so she shook her head obstinately. "No. There's nothing."

Stanley sighed. "Well then. I'll go take that nap."

After her father had padded out of the room, Megan stared at the album lying open on the bed. Delhi. The ruins of an old city, markets, monuments, broken mansions, the zig-zag of roads, the still sad music of times passed. And rising up from it, her mother, wind in her hair, laughing like a witch.

Winter Raga

"Notes can be whimsical, like water. The slightest tilt, and they flow away." Naina pulled the harmonium closer. "And before you know it, you have a new raga."

"Oh shit. Did I not hit the right *re*?"

"Your western music teacher tells you to hit the notes, right? But in Hindustani classical, we won't hit anything."

"Right." Giggling, Vartika examined the chipped nail-polish on Naina's toes. Almost sixteen, and having inherited her father's inquisitive features and her mother's smooth complexion, she was growing up to be a beauty. But she had in her a hearty bonhomie and genuine kindness, traits that Naina found impossible to trace genetically.

"*Rishabh*, yes. But you forgot the *teevra madhyam*," Naina said with a mock-glare, covering her toes with her dupatta. "If *madhyam* becomes *shudh*, the raga will change from Yaman to Bilawal."

"Ya. They both sound so similar though, those two. I mean, not like Yaman and Bhairav, which sound so different."

"Oh, Yaman and Bilawal sound very different too," Naina replied, her face softening. "The *teevra madhyam* is a wilful, dramatic note, not easily ignored. Wait, let me sing the two different ragas for you. Then you can judge for yourself."

The notes spilled forth; lodged deep inside her, like rainwater collected in the cracked roofs of old havelis, their silver trails now ran across the landscape of Naina's life, washing out its colours. And she sang from this exquisite place of runny, dark-light colours, the colours of pain and pleasure, of love and of loss.

Vartika hunched up her knees and listened, clapping like a child when Naina finished. "You're awesome, Naina-didi," she said, hugging her. "I could sit here and listen to you for hours."

"Yaman was my father's favourite raga," Naina said, remembering. "The evening raga."

"Let me try now. I don't know if I can ever be as good as you, but we'll both try."

Naina smiled at the earnest face in front of her. Here was a raw talent that was already overpowering in its intensity, and Naina was sure that, in a few years, the teenager would gain style and sophistication. "You will be much, much better than me," Naina said, taking Vartika's hands in her own. "Just one promise?"

"What?"

"Don't give up classical. I know you're more interested in contemporary music, and you *have* what it takes to really succeed there. If you decide to make music your career, that is. But a solid training in classical will only do you good. The importance of proper *taalim*...never discount that."

"You sound so serious, Didi. What's the matter? Why would I give up classical? My music teacher at school also used to say how important it is, so I literally *forced* Mom and Dad to put out that ad last year, the one to which you'd applied. You're here to teach me, aren't you?"

"Yes, but what if I am not here someday? Your lessons must always continue. In fact, I feel you should enroll in a proper school from next year, take exams, get some certifications."

"Wait...you are going away?" Vartika asked, looking at Naina in surprise.

"I am not going anywhere. I am just saying that in case I ever do..."

"I don't want to talk about it, okay?"

"When you are sixteen, things can seem hard," Naina said softly, putting her arms around the girl. "School, boyfriends, confusion about the future, what college to go to, what to do with one's life..." she continued earnestly. "But you know what I think? I think you are an *amazing* girl and you will have an amazing life, with or without me. Instead of locking yourself up in this room, why don't you spend more time with your parents and your Varun Bhai? And now you have a wonderful sister too, in Karishma..."

Vartika pulled a face. "She's not my sister. I *hate* her. Naina-didi, why can't I go live with you in your house?"

Naina laughed. "In my crumbling old house with barely any electricity and no plumbing? And what would we eat? How would I afford your exorbitant school fees? Your clothes, your parties? Not to mention the court fees, for the abduction case your parents will file!"

"Then what should we do?" Naina's heart warmed at the earnestness of Vartika's face—so child-like and trusting.

"*We* should take our *riyaaz* seriously. We should eat well, and get enough sleep, and study hard for our exams, and think of the wonderful time we will have in college a few years from now."

Vartika nodded. "But don't stop our music lessons, Naina-didi, please?"

"Okay. Now get up quick, quick, it's already dinner time."

"I have homework. I told them to send up my food later.

You're having dinner here tonight, right? I heard Mom ask you earlier. Best of luck!"

✦

By the time Naina went downstairs, another family had just arrived in a whiff of perfume, hugs and half-blown kisses. "So nice you all could make it, so nice, so nice," Neelima gushed.

Naina briefly registered a grey-haired husband and a willowy, fashionably bloused wife. From somewhere between them, a teenaged daughter emerged; pierced eyebrow, spiked hair, chewing gum. "Where's my silly brother?" the girl asked, looking bored. Everyone laughed.

"Aunty, looking fantastic as usual. Each time I see you, I want to ask you about the boutique that does your blouses," Karishma whispered conspiratorially to the woman, who looked pleased.

"We just finished a second round of drinks," Ashok said, rubbing his hands together. "Too bad you three got late."

"You know my dear husband," the woman replied to Ashok, patting her short hair in place. "He got a call from the New York office just as we were leaving."

"I see. How is everything on the work front, Keshav?"

"Everything's great, Ashok. We got a big order from Bloomingdale's. So Varun, are you enjoying your newly married status?"

"Very much, Uncle. Especially some parts of it," Varun replied with a wink, and everyone laughed again.

"By the way, where *is* that brother of yours?" Karishma asked, turning to the girl. "Wasn't he here, like, a moment ago?"

"I think he went up to the study," Neelima said. "Such a studious boy, from childhood. Always first in class."

"And last in everything else," Varun said easily. "*Ladki patana nahin aaya abhi tak*, bloody loser."

"Completely agree. He has no clue how to be popular with the girls," their grey-haired guest said indulgently. "In a few years, his mother and I would love to see him married too, but he just doesn't seem interested. Varun, why don't you have a little chat with him?"

"Enough, guys. Dinner is laid," Karishma said. "*Chalo, chalo*, come Uncle, Aunty, Papa. Mumma has gone out of her way to organise a fab spread. C'mon, Varun."

Naina stood awkwardly in the corner of the hallway, her diminutive form almost hidden by an oversize stone statue of a nude nymphet and around it, a burst of dense, exotic plants. She wanted to step forward and say something bright and light and fashionable, something in their language that would amuse them no end, make her one of them. But her throat was a desert of rough, rasping sands. Water, she needed water. Maybe she could just slink out? The guests were already seated and everyone had forgotten her anyway. Yes, escape, into the cool balmy night, a step backwards, two steps, three—

"Naina!" Karishma swooped down upon her, dragging her into the dining room by the crook of her arm. "Mumma, you forgot! Naina will be joining us for dinner, remember? Everyone, this is Naina. Vartika's music teacher."

"A lovely girl, our Naina," Ashok murmured.

"Lovely," his wife echoed, her eyes bright with alcohol and anticipation.

"Oh, hullo dear," the grey-haired man and his wife said in unison while the daughter looked on curiously.

"Naina, pull up a chair," Karishma said. "And Mumma, won't you send someone to go see where Shekhar is?"

Naina sat down, taking some pulao on her plate and forking it quietly. A servant magically appeared from nowhere and filled her glass with water. Another hovered around the guests, refilling glasses of wine, wiping spills. From the kitchen, the cook sent out endless bowls of food.

"So, Naina, where do you live?" the fashionably-bloused wife asked.

"In Old Delhi. Near Chandni Chowk."

There was a brief silence. "Oh," the wife replied. Another silence. And then, "There he is! Where did you disappear?"

Naina briefly registered a tall young man in jeans, a white kurta and a shy smile. "I'm really sorry," he said, sliding into one of the empty places at the dining table, unfolding his napkin and pouring a glass of water before the servants could do it for him. "There was this fascinating book..."

"Oh puhleez, Shakes, no books," his sister interjected, putting her hands over her ears. "How *typical*. By the way, this is Naina. Naina, this is my retard bro."

"Hi," he said, looking at her intently. "Wasn't it you singing a while back? Glad I came down earlier than these guys, otherwise I would have missed it. It was divine. You are very talented."

"Yup, Shakes, our Naina is very talented," Varun remarked suavely before she could respond. Shekhar reddened, his embarrassment making it evident to Naina that the two men had already discussed her. Biting her lip, she continued to eat.

The conversation at the dining table drifted back to company boards and stock markets. Also, concerts, art exhibitions, foreign trips. *I agree, one can get tired of Paris but never the south of France. And please go to Nice for the Grand Prix, Monaco is lovely, really lovely. And in case you're looking for something outside of the routine London-Paris-New York circuit, try Budapest, so quaint and cultured.*

Such an artful conversation, Naina thought, where everyone is invincible. No mention of the loss of a father, or the struggle to make ends meet, or impossible longings.

✦

The evening was blue, roads like rivers, the undulating ripples of traffic. A muffled wind brushed insistently against the rolled-up windows of the car, making Naina shiver despite the car's crisp heating. Pulling her dupatta closer, she settled back against the upholstered seat and closed her eyes. She was so tired that sleep came immediately, and she began dreaming of stick figures lining up to the beats of a mournful thumri. The taal was *kaherava*, eight beats, *dhaa ge naa tee naa ka dhin naa. Dhaa ge naa tee naa ka dhin naa.* Swathes of white cloth hung from the reedy bodies of the dancers, and their oversized faces were deathly white under the glare of stage lights.

The lights shone like a thousand suns and drops of sweat were breaking out on her forehead. Waking up with a start, she saw that they had entered the old city. In the night, the lone streetlight at the crossing in front of her house burned bright and lantern-like.

"*Aage ki sadak bahut patli hai.*" the driver said, almost accusingly.

Naina nodded, apologetic. He was right; these streets were too narrow for a Mercedes. Stepping out, she thanked him, but he was already reversing the car, perhaps worried that someone might see him in these penniless parts. Barely acknowledging her, he drove away. Her eyes still rimmed with sleep, Naina looked at the disappearing streak of red. How strange it was, she briefly mused, that in all the months she had been involved with Varun, his car had never once come to drop her home. And yet, how apt that she should have been dropped home tonight of all nights. The night she had met Varun with his wife, the night when she had seen the driver's disdain as clearly as she had seen the security guard's pity and an unknown man's embarrassment.

She looked around self-consciously, wondering if anyone else had glimpsed the almost offensive sight of the Mercedes trying to weave its way through the tight grid of roads. But it was almost eleven, all neighbours inside their homes. Well, at least she had one less explanation to give to the world.

Naina unzipped her handbag, pulled out her big bunch of keys and unlocked the door. Then, taking off her sandals, she tiptoed across the courtyard and called out tentatively. "Bua..." No sound, except those from their old transistor. "Bua, are you awake?"

The light was still on in her aunt's room. Naina entered to find her snoring heavily while the transistor by her side belted out a string of advertisements for rubber chappals and herbal cures for acne and impotence. Bending down to turn off first the transistor and then the light, Naina treaded softly out of the room.

In the usual corner of the kitchen, beside a chipped statue of Lord Ganesha, was a steel plate with her share of dinner. She lifted the white muslin to find two chapattis, a small bowl of lentils and a cauliflower sabzi. She was very fond of cauliflower, but for some reason, she felt full tonight. Ah, yes, she'd already had her dinner, hadn't she? Naina screwed her eyes, trying to remember. There had been a pulao of long-grained, fragrant basmati rice, *dum aloo* and yogurt chicken. Other dishes too, that she couldn't recall. And she'd refused dessert—had it been some sort of custard? The one taste still on her tongue was of the pickle—stuffed red whole chillies that had, at one point, brought hot tears streaming down her eyes.

Taking out a steel tumbler from the cupboard, she poured herself some water from an earthen *surahi*. How fiercely Babuji had fought his family when they'd wanted to buy a refrigerator, she recalled. Afterwards, he'd walked Naina into the kitchen and gently explained the cooling effects of the *surahi*. "It may not use sophisticated technology, but sometimes, traditional wisdoms passed down from generation to generation can be so much better. Cheaper, less harmful to the environment. See the graceful arch of its neck, like a swan's? And the smell of earth that perfumes the water, tell me, can the fridge give you that?"

Shaking her head earnestly, twelve-year-old Naina had snuggled down into the crook of her father's elbow. Three years later, she'd snuggled up to him again, instinctively knowing.

Eyes misting, Naina walked out into the courtyard again. Bua had forgotten to put away the *charpai*. Naina remembered her father's last words as he'd lain on that *charpai*: "Thank God I will die in the courtyard of my ancestors' haveli, on a nicely-woven *charpai* under a sky full of stars, instead of in a synthetic bed in a cramped apartment."

Naina sat on the *charpai* and ran her fingers over the ropes, remembering. His skin brittle, his body wasted, yet the eyes holding so much light, the heart so much love. Love for his wife, which he had worn like a talisman through her living years and even after her death. Love for his daughter, the rest of his family, his friends. Babuji...

It was cold, a light grey fog all around, the leaves of the *tulsi* plant curled up in sleep. Naina's breath was smoky, yet she felt warmer than she'd been inside the heated Mercedes. "I've let you down, Babuji, have I not?" she asked gently. "But no more. No more." The silence swirled around her like the waters of the *surahi*, cooling her forehead.

"I can be strong. That's not a problem," she continued earnestly, wiping the dusty wooden knobs of the *charpai* with her dupatta. "The problem is that nothing ever seems to change. Winter comes, then spring, then summer and the rains, followed by autumn and then winter again. The same seasons, the same cycle. Sometimes I feel I will grow old and die here, in this house. You and Amma both gone, Bua still living in the past...memories, just memories. But I want to be young. To have a present, a future."

The stars were faraway pinpoints in the sky, and a soft wind ruffled the tops of the trees adjoining their courtyard. "You remember the magic tricks, Babuji?" Naina said, smiling wistfully into the darkness. "Like when you used to pull a coin out of my ears, or turn a full glass upside down without the water spilling out? Couldn't you do that again? Some magic?"

A dog had started howling just outside their door. "Go away," Naina said, flinging a pebble at the door. "Go home, home."

The dog stopped its yelps, and Naina could hear it limping away, down the narrow, cobbled street and into the heart of the city. The walled city, with its mosques, minarets and the murmurs of old, unsettling stories.

Meeting

Afterwards, Megan would remember small things, like the panelled walls, a clock as lethal as a landmine, the neat, pointless geometry of pens, papers, writing pads. She would remember the wintry spaces between these things, and between her and the Dean of Students, the reedy, thin-lipped man on the other side of the table. The sort of man who has an obliging family, she imagined: wife pretty in her spotless kitchen, children with big plans, well-trained dog, health insurance, tax returns, all filed. The sort of man who stands in front of the mirror every morning to adjust his tie, and thinks I am so-and-so.

The Dean was flanked by the head of Megan's department on one side and an unknown man on the other, and the meeting got off on a false start; handshakes, cups of coffee brought in by a smiling secretary, cookies. Then, the questions.

"Tell us about the procedures you follow with respect to your paperwork," the Dean said.

"With respect to *what*?"

"Your paperwork," he repeated, looking at his watch already. "The e-mail correspondence that you must maintain in case of disruptive students, the record of warnings, the in-person meetings you schedule, the request for third-party adjudication for dispute resolution. In case of a lawsuit..."

"A *lawsuit*," Megan exclaimed, blood rushing to her temples. "But what have I *done*? This is not a sexual harassment case, Dr. Smith!"

"I know what it is *not*, Dr. Adams," he said pointedly. "But it *is* a case of inappropriate conduct by a professor."

"And it is inappropriate conduct to chastise a student for continued misbehaviour in class?" she asked hotly.

"Only if proper procedural guidelines are not followed," he replied levelly. The other two bobbed their heads in unison, like clockwork mice. "A few weeks ago, you reprimanded her in front of the entire class. You should know that students have a right to privacy."

"Her misbehaviour was always in front of the entire class. She was not rude to me in *private*."

"*She* doesn't need to be. Professors do not have a right to privacy." This was the department head. White, very tall, creaseless suit, hair swept back in a severe chignon.

"But the right to privacy refers properly to things like medical conditions—HIV, mental health. It also applies to personal information such as sexual orientation. Even grades. Don't you see how she is *misusing* this clause by threatening legal action?"

"She has a right to explore her options, Dr. Adams. Hence the investigation we've been conducting. And I have to say we have discovered your views about teaching are quite...let us say unconventional."

"There is nothing much to *discover* there," Megan responded tersely. "My resume should have told you that even before you hired me. Critical pedagogy."

"And that explains why you did not document this student's misbehaviour, did not send her any warning letters?"

"Yes. Because I thought it's just a teenager acting out. I thought a good talking-to would suffice. Developing a personal relationship with students and having conversations with them is far more productive than imposing top-down discipline and sending warning notes. It is so important, this idea of community, of collaboration rather than competition between students…don't you see?"

"Oh, we see. But since there's no paper trail to go by, we also see the student's point. She says she never realised you found her classroom behaviour disruptive."

Yeah, right, Megan wanted to say, but she kept silent.

"There were no warnings issued, nothing in writing," the Dean continued. "And suddenly, one day, you embarrassed her in front of the whole class, and next thing she knew, she got a C in her paper. She says she's not been attending class the last few weeks because she feels uncomfortable. She says that's why she decided to lodge a complaint with us. She says—"

"I will be happy to give you her paper to look at. That paper deserved an F," Megan cut in. "I gave that C out of compassion. It seemed from her behaviour that she was going through some problems, and I thought some compassion and a sound scolding would do it, that's all."

"A sound scolding," the Dean said, genuine mirth in his voice. "You forget you are a *professional*, Dr. Adams. Now, just for arguments' sake, could you give us examples of other students you have used the same *fascinating* techniques with, and actually succeeded?"

Megan thought of Segun. The way she'd blasted him when he'd been late for their first tutorial, how he'd hung his head. Never late again, hours of hard work, an A on his most recent paper, his childlike delight when he'd seen it, the way he'd impulsively hugged her – *physical contact is inappropriate,* this committee would probably decree – his promise to work even harder, his impish *now you have to get A in football, Professor*. Megan thought of Liu, who had spent two years in college shrinking from the writing programme because she found the lecturers and their lesson plans too formidable; Liu, with her earnest, entirely untruthful *yes yes yes*, who was finally learning her English watching British and American classics with Megan. *Wuthering Heights*, *Casablanca*, *Roman Holiday* but always returning to her favourite *My Fair Lady*, with Henry Higgins the audacious adjectivore – "*You deliciously low, horribly dirty, presumptuous, impudent, ungrateful, wicked woman*" – and Eliza, his flowergirl, who learned his language and bowed at the ball. Liu, only eight grammatical errors in the last exam, a box of her mother's homemade cookies for Megan afterwards.

Segun, and Liu, and others, so many others: Bill, the Jones girl, Sheetal, Mary, Denice. All of whom would completely unravel in front of this committee. And for what? At the end of it all, the committee would pronounce her methods *inappropriate* – what a quaint word, inappropriate – and direct her to stop. All she needed was another month of tutorials with Segun, a couple more with Liu…

"Dr. Adams? Are there other students you would like us to contact in order to verify your…er…claims of pedagogical success?"

Megan looked away, at the window shades shifting in the breeze. A triangular patch of sun flitted across the hardwood floor, across their impassive features, butterfly-like, now here, now gone, darkening the upper portions of their faces until only mouth-shaped holes remained. "Dr. Adams?"

"No," she said, suddenly making up her mind. "As it is, their lives and their relationships with me have been disrupted enough by this investigation. I am not going to offer any more names and have them subjected to individual harassment."

"In that case, should the student decide to bring a case of bias against you, we will be forced to consider disciplinary action for inappropriate conduct," the voices said. "We will let you know of our decision in writing a few weeks from now. You do realise that we are a *neutral* committee that is not taking any sides for the time being, not until the investigation into your teaching is officially over..."

"I will take your leave now," Megan said, getting up abruptly. "Thank you."

"Another thing, Dr. Adams," the Dean said with a slight smirk. "A matter of some delicacy has come up, has it not..." he continued, turning to the woman on his side.

Megan had already reached the door; she turned and waited. "Yes. It is about your...your *attire*," the head of her department said, her face expressionless. "The flowery skirts, the beads, all that make-up. We don't have a formal dress code as such, but this cannot be appropriate dressing for a professional."

"You mean I should dress like a man," Megan said wearily. *Like you*.

"Please be careful in the future. That is all."

Stepping out of the room and into the corridor, Megan walked to the windows at its furthest end, from where she could get an aerial view of dozens of university buildings rising up in concrete-and-granite solemnity against the skyline. She was suddenly struck by how much they reminded her of companies, or law offices, their stone grey faces silent, obdurate. From her tenth floor perch, the people walking in and out of those wide, heavy buildings looked precariously small. Among them, probably a Pulitzer prize winner, a Guggenheim winner, a future Nobel Laureate, yet all made tiny by those buildings, so tiny.

As Megan turned away from the window and started walking towards the elevator, her eyes fell on a cluster of framed black and white photographs of the university from earlier times. 'Convocation, School of Arts and Sciences, 1955,' one read, and another said 'Speech by City Counselor, University Square, 1968.' There were half a dozen others, of people with camera-smiles fixed on their faces against a backdrop of the university. Individuals and institutions, picture perfect. The people were all old now, many probably even dead. But the buildings, they remained.

✦

She tried to put it out of her head for the rest of the week, focusing on her lesson plans, lectures, weekly tutorials, groceries, utility bills instead. But Saturday evening, on the train ride back to Princeton, a high breeze carried it all back to her. As stations pulsed past, their names carried by speeding black-on-yellow signs – Elizabeth, Linden, Metchuchen, Metropark, Edison, New Brunswick – the voices from that meeting sounded again, again, and she could hear the shuffling of notepads, feet, the precise ticking of the wall-clock.

She looked out of the train window at the passing automobile shops, the broken streets, houses squatting fatly in grids. A few miles later, a stone bridge; underneath it a river, its copper-coloured water thick with reeds. And quite suddenly, she found herself wondering about the modernity whose cause she so passionately espoused in and out of class. A modern world, with so many choices for women, yet still very much a man's world, with little place for compassion or community or flowery skirts. No, it was a world of business suits and lawsuits, of committees and careful conversations.

Getting off at Princeton, Megan collected her mussed-up hair into a ponytail and hailed a cab. She hadn't told her father she was coming; it was to be a surprise. As the cab left the townhouses of Princeton behind and turned into the quieter, green-lined lanes of Pennington, her mind began churning again. What had that quiet student said last month, about how three generations of women laughed and cooked together in their oversized kitchen? Megan could almost imagine them now, their plump faces bent over the cooking range, the bawdy jokes that would flavour their food marvellously. After that girl graduated and became a *professional* – a male word, in a male world – she would enjoy the income, identity, and independence that generations of women before her had fought so hard for. And in the process, she would have to abdicate that tight community of women, its horrors, its insights so opaque to the outside world, its own female freedoms.

✦

"You should have told me they were coming, Dad."

"Well, I didn't know *you* were coming! And Jeff called just *five* minutes back to say he and Angela will be dropping by. It's Children's Day for me," Stanley replied with a smile, bending over the fireplace to stoke the embers, his cheeks ruddy from the blaze. The dry logs burned crisply, but there was some wet wood in the pile which sizzled and sent up a lot of smoke. "How do you like the first fire of the winter?"

"It's too early! Agreed there's a slight nip in the air, but whoever needs a fire in November?"

"Some of us do. Early fires, to warm our bones," Stanley joked, shaking his head when Megan didn't reply. "What's the matter? You're the one who complains that Jeff doesn't check on me nearly as often as he should."

"I know, I know," Megan said, getting up from the sofa. "It's just that I've had a difficult week, and I really don't feel too talkative."

"Jeff is hardly very talkative himself," Stanley laughed. "Besides, they're only coming for a drink, not dinner. So stop pouting. He *is* your brother, you know."

"And I love him, you know that. Look, why don't I go up to my room. I'll come down and say hi to them later, I promise."

"Sure. Otherwise I can just tell them you've had a rough week. And oh, darling—forgot to tell you. Kevin said he might drop by too."

"Kevin said that?" Megan asked, smiling for the first time that week. "He didn't say anything to *me*. It'll be really nice to see him."

Megan went up to her bedroom, delighting, at once, in the smell of freshly laundered sheets and the sachets of lemon balm. Outside, the light was fading, and she opened the window to breathe in the high silence of the pines. *This house is an oasis*, she thought, pulling off her jeans and climbing into bed to savour the stillness of dusk with a guilty *I will close my eyes for just a moment*. But she had barely slept that entire week, and soon she found herself being swept away, away, through floating pines, moon-silvered clouds, lakes slurping at the edges, and a rough wind whittling through it all, drying them up until all that remained was Angela's arid laugh…

"Wake up, you idiot!"

"Huh?" Megan peeped out sleepily from under her covers. "…Kevin?"

"Welcome to terra firma. It's *eight*," Kevin said, standing tall, his sandy hair combed back neatly. His sharp nose and square chin had always given him a sensible air, but Megan knew he could be quite a softy. When they were both freshmen at Princeton, they had come across a dead kitten run over on the road. Kevin had given it a decorous burial; afterwards, she'd caught him crying.

"Remember that kitten?" Megan asked, sitting up in bed, hair tousled.

"You crazy woman, you've been sleeping for over two hours! Jeff and Angela came and went. I have to go too."

"I dreamt of Angela's laugh," Megan said, rubbing her eyes. "Can you pass me my jeans, please?"

"That was no dream. Angela was in very good spirits; she was finding all her own jokes really funny. Such trying laughter that woman has. Like a duck in orgasm. Here, your jeans. Wait, you *naked* underneath?"

"Shut up," Megan murmured. "And who gave you the right to enter a lady's room without first knocking?"

"The door would have broken if I had knocked any louder, *lady*," Kevin shot back, grinning to see her trying to struggle into her jeans underneath the duvet. Then his face became serious. "Stanley mentioned you'd had a rough week. The meeting not go too well?"

Megan shook her head. "A lot depends on the outcome of their investigation, I guess. Till then, they're neutral, they said. Hell, they were talking about a possible lawsuit."

"Neutral, my foot. And wait—a lawsuit? What the hell. It's not like it's a sexual harassment case or something!"

Megan laughed. "You know, that's exactly what I had said."

"It's unbelievable, all this mental stress they're putting you through. You should be suing *them*!" Kevin said, pacing around the room. "But hey, I think it'll all die down after a while. They might take some internal disciplinary action, but I doubt it will go any further than that."

"You think so?" Megan asked, her face hopeful. When Kevin nodded, she smiled gratefully. "And you know the saddest thing? I really try to make a difference to these students' lives. I bring them food, and tell them stories, and..." Megan's eyes welled up, and she looked away.

"I know you do," Kevin said softly, coming to sit on the bed by her side and tucking a stray wisp of hair behind her ear.

"I'm being *ridiculous*," Megan said, a tear rolling down her cheek. "Tears are so uncharacteristic of me, but this year..."

"Shhsh, it's fine." He put his arm around her. "It will all work out. I just hope you don't regret any of your decisions because of this one incident."

Megan snuggled closer, into his old, familiar smell of soap and sweat and baseball. "What decisions?"

"Of going to Newark. Of deciding to be an academic, even."

"Of course not. Not for a moment," she replied. "But it's certainly made me think about how universities are becoming more and more like corporations. We are the provider of services, competing against other companies for profit. The students are consumers, the syllabus is a legal contract, and if the consumers don't like the service, they take their business elsewhere. No idealism, no space for individuality and eccentricity, just a business model of professionalism..."

"Yes, but don't let this period of trial get you down too much, okay?" Kevin said, running his fingers through her hair. "You've just had a tough year, what with your jerk ex-boyfriend, and then the move to Newark, and now this."

Megan sighed. "I had thought William and I were two peas in a pod, remember?"

"Yup. Too bad he was a busted pea," Kevin said agreeably. "Listen, you need a break. Why don't you come with me to Beijing?"

"To *Beijing*? You're taking a trip to China? Oh yes, I forgot. Your firm was looking at offshoring some operations, right?"

"More than just offshoring. We're expanding in fairly substantial ways, with give and take on both sides. I'll be travelling there in December, for a couple of weeks. Wanna go?"

"Dunno," Megan replied, wiping her eyes with her sleeves. "We'll see. Your colleague Kim, is he going too? His family is originally from China, right?"

"Like, three generations ago. He's never been there his entire life. I doubt what he has learnt about China from his grandparents would be of much use in the context of China today."

"Yes, diasporas are probably a thing of the past, the ancient homeland versus the land of exile. Now the globe is shrinking so close we all need to be travellers, at home anywhere in the world."

"Yeah, I guess that's an interesting perspective, and probably very true."

"And why are you looking at me like that?"

"I just realised how beautiful you look. Even without make-up," Kevin said softly.

"Yes, *gorgeous*," Megan joked, suddenly uncomfortable.

"And your eyes. At eight, I used to think they were the most beautiful eyes I'd ever seen," he continued, tracing a finger along her jawline. "I still do."

She sucked in her breath. Something had been changing between them for some time now, slowly, imperceptibly, like the shifting colours of sea, pale blue to startling turquoise. To rolling russet, as sea met sky, the distant heat of its horizon. A table lamp was casting an orange glow and the evening threatened to sizzle, unlit embers everywhere.

"Lately you've started behaving funny, you know that?" she asked, deliberately keeping her voice light.

He was still swimming in the green depths of her eyes, looking for a child and finding only woman. Then he kissed her, full on the mouth, not cutely like they used to as children, but deeply, insistently, seeping into her.

"Kevin!" she spluttered, finally coming up for breath. "What are you *doing*? Are you out of your freakin' mind? You are my best friend, for God's sake!"

"That's what you've always wanted, haven't you?" he snapped, gripping her shoulder tightly. "Kevin for everything, except when it comes to falling in love! For that you have ..."

"Stop, please stop," she whispered.

"I'm sorry," he said, instantly contrite. "It's just that—" And he pulled her close and kissed her again, ravenously, and she suddenly found herself closing her eyes and kissing him back, her hands in his hair, on his neck, on his hard, hard chest. And his hands were on her, all of her, and then he swore and was on his feet just as quickly. "Shit," he muttered, his blue eyes almost as cloudy as her green ones. "I have to go."

"We should talk," she said shakily. "This is *crazy*. I don't even know what's going on in my life anymore. Where are you *going*?"

"Later," he said, almost running out of the room. At the door, he looked back. "I'm sorry, Meg," he said quietly. "I don't know what came over me. I do have feelings for you that go beyond friendship, guess I always have. But if you don't, well, I respect that. I value your friendship, I do. Will behave myself in the future."

✦

After he'd left, Megan got out of bed and walked to the window on wobbly legs. Beyond the lone street lamp's mellow ring of light, it was pitch dark, night-coloured shapes everywhere. Far away a vixen's wail, somewhat closer a scampering of several hooves, most likely deer settling in for the night.

Megan could see at least two pairs of animal eyes, and she experienced a sudden urge to leave everything behind and escape into the woods, tail flashing.

"Megan?" her father hollered from downstairs. "Aren't you coming down for dinner?"

"Not hungry," she yelled back. "But I'll come down and give you company."

Stanley was slicing bread on the kitchen counter. "Jeff and Angela didn't stay for dinner. A good thing, considering there wasn't much in the house."

"What's this?" Megan murmured. "Chicken salad?"

"Yes. Kevin threw it together with last night's leftover chicken. And he brought my favourite French bread. Funny he didn't stay for dinner. I hope you two didn't fight?"

"No. Everything's fine. He probably remembered something important."

"That's what he said. Well. Why don't you have this bread with some stinky cheese? No, don't shake your head—you must eat something."

"You behave like I am thirteen, not thirty," Megan complained, taking a bite off the crusty bread.

"Sometimes you *behave* like you're thirteen," Stanley countered indulgently, opening the fridge to take out the cheese and a half-empty bottle of wine. "Sleeping at odd times, red eyes, no food. What's going on?"

"My meeting at the university didn't go too well," Megan replied tersely. *And my meeting with my best friend didn't go too well either, but never mind.*

"I'm sorry to hear that. Want to talk about it?" Stanley asked gently, pouring two glasses of wine.

"Not really," Megan said. "Don't worry, Dad, I'll handle it. I've been a bit of a weeping willow lately, lots of bad decisions. But that's about to change.

"About time too," Stanley replied, staring at her intently from above his glasses like a dragonfly.

Megan blushed. "Stop it," she said uncomfortably. "I know what you're thinking, but don't. For the hundredth time, Kevin and I are just..."

"All right, all right," her father grinned. "How's the wine?"

Megan took a sip of the pale amber liquid and rolled it around her tongue. "Ah, *nice*. When did you get this?"

"Last week." Stanley ladled a big helping of chicken salad onto his plate. "Sure you don't want some of this?"

"Well, since Kevin made it, maybe I'll have just a little," Megan replied, smiling wanly.

"Let's go sit outside on the porch for a bit, shall we?" Stanley asked, once they had finished doing the dinner dishes. "By this time next month, it will be freezing."

"Sure," Megan said, strolling outside with her glass of wine. They sat in companionable silence, staring into the far distance: the starless sky, the moon with its cold blue light, the trees lost in darkness. "Kevin was saying I need a break," she said after a while. "He asked me to fly to Beijing with him next month."

"Well, I suppose it's as good a place as any other. And you do have your winter break coming up in December."

"Yes. But I was thinking if I do have to travel halfway across the world, what's wrong with my original idea?"

"What idea?"

"India. Remember, I said I might go to India."

Stanley looked at his daughter carefully. "Ah, yes. You did mention it."

"So? What do you think?"

Stanley was quiet for a few moments. Then he exhaled deeply. "Now that I think about it, I don't see why not. You've travelled on your own before, even if not so far away…I think you'll be fine."

"Don't tell me you were worried about my *safety*," Megan laughed.

"That too. One reads stuff in the papers. It seems different now than it was, when your mother and I were there," Stanley said, reflecting. "Speaking of which, I will write to a lady your mother knew well in Delhi. Her name was Shakuntala. Maybe you might want to meet her?"

"Would love to. Thanks, Dad."

"You're welcome. How long would you be gone for?"

"About two weeks, I think. If I go mid-December, I can get back by New Year's."

Stanley nodded. "Well, Meg. If you've decided to go to India after all, and to meet your mother's friends," he said, lacing his fingers, "there is something else I should probably tell you."

Excerpts from a Diary

Today one of Shakuntala's friends came to visit her. The friend was in her seventh month; she wore a loose kameez and looked quite rosy. Now Shakuntala is very upset, and won't say why. She stands quietly in the kitchen, making her fabled shampoo. The *reetha*, *amla* and *shikakai* have been soaking overnight; now she will boil the mixture, mash it to a pulp and strain it into a bottle. I am endlessly fascinated by Shakuntala's tins and jars and bottles, into which she pounds and mashes all manner of roots and fruits and barks and berries.

"Is it because your friend is already married and you are not?" I ask gently. Today I am wearing a sari and the pleats keep unravelling down my middle.

Shakuntala glares at me and says something I cannot understand.

"What is *amla*?" I ask quickly, to change the subject.

"Indian gooseberry," she says. "Sour, like lime."

"Can I have one?" I ask. I don't like limes, but I always want to eat anything I have not eaten before.

"Go ask your husband," Shakuntala says spitefully. "And take off that stupid sari! And why are you always in my house anyway?" She has switched back to Hindi and is speaking too fast, but I can tell this is what she means.

I sit down cross-legged on the kitchen floor. Dusk has begun to fall, mauve shadows everywhere. Birds are flying home in straight black lines, and the sky is all dots and stripes. I know I will soon have to return home too. "Marriage is not always great, you know," I say in English. "You could end up marrying someone you don't love, or someone who doesn't love you. Can you imagine what that would be like? Lying flushed in the same bed, waiting for him to turn to you? Waiting for a smile, a touch, a simple word of kindness... waiting, always waiting, while the hole in your heart keeps getting bigger."

Shakuntala, of the indigo-stained hands, has left her shampoo-making to join me on the kitchen floor. Her eyes hold questions for me; I see how my language shuts her out too.

"When I saw your friend, you know what I thought?" I ask her softly, enunciating each word with clarity. "That I would also like to have a baby."

She nods and looks away. For the next few minutes, we are both quiet while our unborn children gurgle inside us. "Boy or girl?" She asks me then.

"Oh, girl. I want a girl," I say without hesitation.

"What your daughter be when...grow up? Teacher? Doctor?" Shakuntala asks me, clasping my soft large hands in her tiny blue ones. In that moment, she is my sister and our hearts want to heal.

"A traveller," I say with a smile. "I want her to not confine herself. Not to a house, not to a city, not to a country. No, I want her to travel the whole world and seek out her own truths. And someday, I want her to come see India."

Rich and Poor

It had been a long, leaden flight. Megan got up and stretched, her head missing the loosely hanging lip of the overhead luggage compartment by inches. Ever since the *Fasten your Seatbelts* sign had stopped flashing, the bangs and thuds of suitcases and the screech of luggage wheels had turned the aircraft into a jumble of jostling hips, elbows, and infants' screams. Stiff-necked, dubious of her own aptitude in elbowing, Megan waited until most of the aircraft had emptied before wheeling out her suitcase and laptop bag through the aisle.

Walking into the airport, the knowledge that this was no longer America sat namelessly inside her; no, this was India, ten thousand miles away from home. The slick images from the travel agency's *Exotic India* brochure – a ruby-coloured sun sliding up the Himalayan slopes, the shifting sands of Rajasthan, the marbled, moonlit glory of the Taj Mahal, the palm fronds framing the oily, glistening waters of Kerala, Delhi's famed red sandstone forts – had all evaporated over the course of the fifteen-hour flight. In its place was a clotted feeling in her stomach that translated, more immediately, into a desperate desire for a bed and eight uninterrupted hours of sleep.

The terminal was all lights, lush carpeting, art on the walls. Looking around, Megan saw cafés selling gourmet foods, a spa, and well-dressed women and men milling about with laptops and iPods. A far cry from the pre-modern Third World of the American media, she thought wryly. It was very early morning, hers being the only international flight that had arrived around that time. She had not checked any baggage in either, wanting to travel light, and immigration formalities took very little time. Her papers were examined by a man in his late fifties, bald as a stone, and with an extra mouthful of teeth.

"Welcome to India, dear madam," he said, his broad smile displaying his dental works to full advantage. "Work or vacation?"

"Vacation," she said, smiling back. "It's my first visit to your country."

"The first of many times, we hope." He stamped her papers energetically. "Wish you a very pleasant stay. And if you need any help, please ask any of the airport personnel. Taxis, hotels, tourism, currency exchange, all information available."

Behind Megan, a woman was speaking loudly. "Hope the day comes when they learn to treat South Asian passport holders as politely at international borders. There we are all terrorists, the lot of us!"

"Shhh, quiet," the husband said, smiling apologetically at Megan.

Megan thanked the immigration official, winked at the husband, and quickly wheeled her luggage away. Exchanging five hundred dollars into Indian rupees at a Thomas Cook counter, she walked across to the pre-paid taxi booth and drew out a folded sheet of paper from her pocketbook. "Hi! I'd like a cab to this hotel, please. I have a reservation there," she said to the young boy at the counter, smiling.

The boy took the sheet of paper from her and smiled back. "Sure, Ma'am."

"How is the hotel? Safe?" she asked him.

"Yes, very safe," he replied, glancing at the name. "One of the best hotels in the city, Ma'am. Very expensive also. But maybe not too expensive when you pay in dollars...?"

"Oh no, it's expensive regardless of the currency," Megan replied tersely, thinking of how much this two-week trip to India was costing her.

"At least you will spend your holidays in the lap of luxury and maybe meet your Prince Charming." The boy looked so upbeat Megan had to laugh.

"That would be nice, but if you don't get me a taxi soon, I will go to sleep right here."

"Out of the airport and to the right," he said with a grin, handing her a yellow slip. "You'll see a line of blue cabs with the company name. Your number is 14. Show the man in the white uniform this slip, and he'll help you. Two hundred fifty rupees, please."

She walked out of the airport and right into swirls of fog, a lifting breeze nipping sharply at her throat. Dawn was just breaking, and it was like an early winter morning in any city around the world: the sun not yet out, licks of grey cloud, the sky pink and moist. And it was cold, colder than she'd expected. "Delhi," Megan murmured, pulling her coat closer.

Sitting in the cab minutes later, she found her mind making other journeys, through parallel worlds past and present, of things that did happen, or could have. As she began to doze off, the one thought that rose up from that crisscrossed landscape of myth and memory like a shimmering, insistent peak was this: *Dad wants me to find out.*

✦

"Madam—"

Megan woke up with a jerk. The cab had glided smoothly into a driveway, and two pairs of eyes were upon her. The driver got out, arranged her luggage on a trolley and held the door open for her. Still groggy, she tipped the driver.

Walking into the hotel, her numbed senses registered a towering archway, expanses of polished marble, the tinkle of chandeliers, a waterfall. Fresh, unnamed flowers lingered lightly in the air, and distant strains of music mingled soothingly with the gurgles of the water. "It's all lovely," she said, presenting her passport at the check-in desk, "but I really must go to bed."

"Not a problem, Dr. Adams," the smartly-dressed woman said in a formal tone, looking up her registration information with a smile. "International flights can be very exhausting. We've taken a copy of your passport and visa; all other formalities can wait. The bell-boy will escort you to your room. Have a wonderful stay."

In the elevator, the gangly bell-boy kept stealing glances at her from time to time. He seemed to be about eighteen and had a big homey pimple on his nose. "What's your name?" she asked kindly. "Pappu," he replied, turning red.

Her room was on the tenth floor. After her luggage had been deposited, she gave Pappu a thousand rupees – around twenty dollars, she calculated – and his wide, astonished grin told her it was more than he usually received. After he'd left, she walked to the floor-to-ceiling windows on the city-facing side and looked out at the white-gold skyline, the domes and turrets, the tops of trees, the city pregnant with secrets.

"Later, later," she murmured, peeling off her clothes, unzipping her suitcase and pulling out her pajamas. As she slid between the covers and laid her head on the fluffed-up pillows, the last thought on her mind was of hundreds of pigeons flying in tandem, their downy feathers all around.

She woke up feeling whole again. The clock on the bedside table said two. Two in the afternoon in India...hell, that would be around five in the morning back home. She'd slept for *seven hours*. Oh well. She lifted her legs out of the buttersoft bed and padded up to the windows again. It was quite sunny for a winter afternoon, and much too promising to be wasted in any more sleep.

Rubbing her eyes, she looked around the room with more interest than she'd been able to muster when she'd first stepped in, and noted the king-size bed with sheets that must boast a sky-high thread count, the tall and characterful windows, the framed, embroidered silks adorning the walls, even a massage chair. More high points in the bathroom: a sunken bathtub, candles, Egyptian towels, and a wooden cabinet with vials of scrubs, body butters, clay masks, rosewater. "Oh well," she said again, in sweet surrender.

For the next hour, Megan scrubbed and soaked and primped and pampered herself in scented water while soft channel music filtered into the bathroom. Afterwards, her skin poreless and petal-fresh, she slipped into a bathrobe and padded back into the bedroom to take out her diary and dial a number. Three rings, four rings, five—and then a woman's voice.

"Hullo, my name is Megan Adams. I've reached India. Am I speaking to Shakuntala?"

✦

This time Megan was able to notice all the details in the lobby, like the raw silk upholstery, the exquisite weave of the carpets, the wood painstakingly polished to a gleam. It was crowded now, lobby managers attending to guests, the click of high heels across the marble, the intermittent rings of cellphones, a child's sudden whimper. But business combined well with beauty within those walls, with people speaking in hushed tones, everything tranquil. What a strange thing it is, Megan mused, this power of a mere *building*, whether a university or a hotel, to subdue.

A massive waterfall at the end of the lobby drew her in, and she walked across to the boulders over which it cascaded. The water was collecting in a tiled blue pool at the base, with bits of algae and colourful fish. The cooling spray over her face made her close her eyes with pleasure and think briefly of home. Not the Princeton house where she'd grown up but, surprisingly, the new one in Pennington, with cardinals and swallows' nests, and the russet shades of dusk and dawn, and her father standing smilingly at the door in his apron.

I miss you, Dad, and I don't know what the hell I'm doing here, she thought with a sudden pang of guilt.

"Did you sleep well, Dr. Adams?" the girl at the reception asked pleasantly.

"Yes, very well, thank you. Can we complete the rest of the paperwork now?"

"Sure. Would you also like a tour of the hotel? We have indoor as well as outdoor swimming pools, gymnasiums, sports rooms, tennis court, an *ayurvedic* spa, restaurants serving a variety of cuisines—you would really like *Malabar*..."

"I would *love* a tour of the hotel. Tomorrow, if that's okay? Today I wanted to go explore the city a bit, someplace I can look at authentic Indian handicrafts...pottery, and textiles, small artifacts maybe?"

"There are many places like that nearby. I will ask the concierge to advise you on options. Also, he can arrange tours for you, day tours in and around Delhi as well as overnight ones to other parts of India."

There goes whatever remained of my money. "Awesome," Megan said, rested and reckless.

Sitting in the cab, she was able to see the city for the first time. Outside of the five-star lull, life looked different. She saw thinly-clothed men pushing carts of vegetables along the shiny, serrated edge of the road, children with spindly legs and chapped lips selling glamorous posters of filmstars, the poor huddling under the city's massive bridges and flyovers, their threadbare blankets drawn close in anticipation of a rough winter evening.

The first time the cab stopped at a traffic light, a grimy boy who couldn't have been a day more than eight ran up and pressed his face against the window. A thick green glob of snot was pushing its way out of his nose and he sucked it back, flashing Megan a broken-toothed grin and holding up his packets of handkerchiefs for her to see. Megan rolled down the windows and smiled at him. "How much?" she asked him in English, looking to the driver for translation.

"*Pachaas*," the boy replied, still grinning. The answer prompted a volley of abuses from the cab driver, upon which the boy stuck his tongue out and said "*Bees*."

"Twenty rupees, madam," the driver said, turning to Megan with a satisfied look. "Earlier he say fifty. Always high for foreigner."

"Well, I'm not sure I need handkerchiefs, but I'll take them anyway," she said, taking the money out of her pocketbook. "At least he is trying to work, not begging."

The next one was. She had two unruly braids, a sweater with a big hole and bare feet. Megan saw her snaking her way through the traffic and tapping on the windows of the more expensive cars. A Mercedes directly in front of them rolled down its gleaming windows to give her some money, and it must have been more than she'd expected, for she gave a sudden whoop of joy and would probably have taken the rest of the day off were it not for a woman who suddenly materialised from nowhere, gave the girl a solid cuff across her ear, took the money and pushed her in the direction of the other cars.

It was a difficult sight, and Megan couldn't help thinking of the women she had encountered back in the lobby of the hotel; women in pearls and silks, who walked in whiffs of perfume and wheeled expensive strollers. And she was reminded of the million-dollar homes of Princeton and the homelessness of Newark, and of how, beyond the elaborate, arbitrary politics and economics that had divided the world up into blocks, zones and hemispheres, the division between the rich and the poor still remained the most vital, the most resounding.

✦

The handicrafts market that the concierge had insisted she visit – *no matter what you decide beforehand, Ma'am, you will ultimately buy many things,* he'd predicted gravely – was a modern, beautifully designed bazar with shops from different states of India. From the moment she entered through the patterned gates, Megan was enthralled. On display were hand embroidered cottons and fine silks, beaded purses, gems and glassware, figurines of brass and terracotta, furniture made out of bamboo and carved wood, paintings depicting the range of artistic traditions of the country. The sheer breadth of choices was making her dizzy, and she felt like a deer wandered away from the woods and onto a road ablaze with hundreds of headlights.

"When in doubt, start with a good meal," said a voice behind her, and she turned to find an elderly man with a long white beard looking at her with interest.

"Ah, always a good idea, especially when one is as starved as I am. Except that the choices there are infinite too," she said with a laugh, gesturing towards the long line of food stalls.

"So let's start with the basics," he replied, eyes twinkling. "Have you eaten Indian food before? I'm Singh, by the way. Balbir Singh."

"Megan Adams. Pleased to meet you," she said, extending her hand. "And of course," she replied, once the handshake was over. "Who in the world hasn't eaten Indian food? I've had chicken tikka masala and *chhole* and *baingan bharta* and aloo gobi and naan bread!"

"That's great," he said encouragingly. "It means you have sampled a few dishes from Punjab, one of our northern states. So, even though there are several hundred more dishes in that state alone, we can steer you away from the Punjab stall for now, so you can try the food of one of the other states..."

"And how many states does India have again?"

"Twenty-eight for now," he replied cheerfully. "And each has several culinary traditions, with some traditions cutting across state boundaries. The good news is that not all culinary traditions are represented here, so that does narrow your choices a little bit."

She laughed. "I'll say. So now that you've made me look like a complete idiot, why don't you come straight out and tell me what to eat?"

"Gladly, my dear," he said, tucking his arm through hers companionably. "How about some Hyderabadi biryani, with mutton *raan*?"

"Oh, actually I've eaten biryani before..." Megan began timidly, only to be cut short with an imperious wave of his hand.

"Did you know biryani was invented in the kitchens of the Mughal sultanate? There are many kinds of biryani—Hyderabadi, Awadhi, Bohri, Malabari…"

"Why don't you just shoot me and be done with it," Megan muttered, to be rewarded with a loud guffaw.

"Feisty, aren't we. Okay, so let's not do biryani. What about some South Indian food? The best known is the vegetarian stuff—dosas, idli, vada, *utthapam* – but the real jewels are their non-vegetarian preparations, the spicy fish, the crab, the many kinds of cured muttons. Or you could try Bengali cuisine. Mustard fish, shrimp in coconut curry, potatoes in poppy seed paste, fried pumpkin flowers. And in case you're looking for comfort food, I would suggest the momos from the north-eastern states' stalls—they're steamed chicken or pork dumplings, and they serve it with red chilli paste…"

"Enough, enough," Megan said with a grin. "What a speech to inflict on an unsuspecting tourist! Listen, why don't you join me for lunch, and order for both of us? And maybe you can help me plan my travel itinerary too. I want to head to the Himalayas for some ice-skating next week. Should I go to Shimla or Mussoorie?"

✦

Megan dragged all her bags and baskets into the lobby, earning a nod of approval from the portly concierge. After a very satisfying lunch with her chance friend, from whom she had learnt a lot more about Indian cultures and cuisines, she had shopped for over three hours. For herself, she'd picked up an embroidered Kashmiri *phiran*, jute flip-flops embellished with mirrors, and an intricately carved sandalwood trinket-case. For her father, she'd got two woollen shawls along with a small, exquisite carpet for his library, and for Kevin, a set of hand-painted silk ties. She'd also bought some expensive tableware from the glass shop for Jeff and Angela, thoroughly regretting that decision on the way back to the hotel; the delicate cut-glass plates and bowls would never make it unscathed on the long, bumpy flight home. Still, it had been a day well-spent, and all she wanted now was to smear on a clay mask and soak her feet in the tub.

Pappu the bell-boy came forward shyly. "I take to your room," he said, not looking at her directly.

"Thank you so much," Megan said, recognising all too well the signs of a teenage crush and handing him her bags with an amused smile.

Waving at the coiffured ladies at the reception, she had just begun walking towards the elevator when the lobby manager came up to her, sari pinned high. "You have a guest, Dr. Adams."

"I do? I wasn't expecting anyone this evening…"

"Yes, the lady did say you were expecting her tomorrow, but that she decided to come today. We told her we did not have information on what time you'd be back, but she said she would be happy to wait. She's been waiting for close to an hour."

"Oh, she must be Shakuntala," Megan exclaimed half to herself, flustered. "Never mind—where is she?"

"In the seating area behind the waterfall," the manager replied, pointing discreetly. "Would you like me to send some coffee for you?"

"Yes, that would be great. No, wait, maybe I'll ask her to come up to my room, and order room service," she said with a distracted smile, her eyes scanning the far end of the lobby and the elderly figure half-hidden by a pillar.

She was tiny, five feet two at the most, bunched in a black shawl like a bird. Megan saw her fluttering her bony fingers over the silk upholstery of the *diwan* she sat on. But when Megan came closer, she saw to her surprise that her guest was not old at all; no, she was very young, even if quite frail.

"Hi, I'm Megan," she said, walking up and extending her hand in confusion.

"Hello," the young woman replied, standing up. She was very light-skinned, with soft green eyes. Underneath her shawl she wore a salwar-kameez, and her toes were uncovered despite the chill outside. She looked ill at ease, the smattering of veins in her temple throbbing bluely.

"No, sit, sit, please. I'm sorry I don't quite understand...I mean, I was expecting a lady called Shakuntala. You couldn't possibly—"

"No," the woman replied quickly. "Shakuntala is my aunt. She couldn't come, so she sent me instead. My name is Naina."

Old City

"What do you mean you couldn't ask her?" Shakuntala grumbled, resting her head on a dimpled elbow and spreading herself amply over the *charpai*. She was shelling peas in preparation for lunch, and she threw fistfuls of them into her mouth instead of into the steel bowl on her lap while the pods collected in a basket below. "Isn't that why you had gone to meet her yesterday? *Insisted* on going, even though I said I would go myself today! Why couldn't you ask her straight away?"

"She seemed very nice, Bua," Naina replied, pulling her shawl closer and blowing on her palms for warmth. A fog hung dense and low over the courtyard, turning their words into fluty whispers of white. If they were lucky, small dots of sunlight would dance around the courtyard later in the day, and the tight leaves of the *tulsi* would uncurl. If, on the other hand, today turned out to be as cold as yesterday, she would really have to think about buying that room heater...

"Really? And how is that?" Shakuntala's eyes blazed like a monster's, and armies of peas groaned and disappeared into her green-tongued, unrelenting mouth without a fight.

"I mentioned I hadn't eaten lunch, so she took me to her room and ordered biryani for me. Such a beautiful hotel, Bua. And she gave me a pair of her own woollen socks to wear.

And the fact that she had me dropped home in a taxi because it was getting late…“

“Oh, this and that, this and that. Biryani! Hotels! Woollen socks! Taxi rides to Timbuktoo! Like we can't even afford socks and taxis! Like every good-for-nothing passerby will take pity on us, fling a few *paisas* our way and make us wallow in gratitude! Oh, if it hadn't been for that idiot father of yours who left us nothing…"

"Bua…"

"Okay, okay, your father was a king and he left us so much we don't know what to do with it. Happy? And now you've gone and invited this girl for dinner on Saturday! Nonsense, I say!"

"It's just dinner; Megan understands our circumstances. She's not going to expect anything fancy. Anyway, I think it has been more than a year since we invited anyone for a meal."

"Keep quiet! You want us to throw feasts and banquets like the courtesans? Hang up sequined curtains and spray jasmine *ittar* to welcome guests every evening, serve biryani and nahari for dinner, and feed them paan off a silver platter afterwards? With what, I ask? All the buried treasures your father has left for us? And understands our circumstances, does she? I will show that *gori*. You wait and watch."

"Bua, please don't," Naina said, getting up to sit next to Shakuntala on the *charpai*. "She just wants to meet and talk to you, that's all…"

"*Achcha*, *she* wants! You want, your father wants, your mother wants, your grandmother wants, the Prime Minister of the country wants! Always, always. I say, what about what I want? Tell me, what about that?"

"What do you want, Bua?" Naina asked wearily.

"I want that girl's mother to return what is rightfully ours!" Shakuntala shouted.

"Bua, Bua, Megan's mother is dead, and I am not sure if she even *knows* about... what's the matter? What happened??"

Shakuntala had gone very quiet. "Dead?" she whispered hollowly. "Her mother is *dead*?"

"Yes...why, didn't you know?" Naina asked, confused. "Her father wrote you that letter...I read it out to you, remember? He said..."

"I know what he said," Shakuntala snapped. "He said the girl was visiting India and wanted to meet me. There was nothing in the letter about her mother's death."

"But you knew her mother! Didn't you know she was dead?" asked Naina, puzzled.

Shakuntala had closed her eyes. Opening them a few moments later, she stared at the winter sky.

"No. No, I didn't," she muttered. "We did not stay in touch after she went back to America. I did not even have her address."

"Oh. I see. That explains a lot." Naina said slowly. "You know, when she spoke of her mother's death, I wondered why you hadn't ever mentioned it in all these years. But listen, how did her father have our address?"

"Stop asking stupid questions, girl! *I* did not have their address. *They* had ours," her aunt replied, irritated. "We have always lived in this same house."

"Oh yes, I had forgotten that," Naina said softly. "Bua, I am very happy I invited her for dinner. Just cook a simple meal, chat with her for a while. She wants to talk about her mother, I think. And then we can ask her to return what you've been hankering for. It's much better this way, and everyone gets something."

"*Theek, theek*," Shakuntala muttered under her breath. "You think you have all the answers. Just like your father. You will need to do some shopping for the dinner."

"I already got you spices for the entire month, and we have enough rice, potatoes and onions. Eggs too, I think. And these peas, or whatever will be left of them once you're done. If you need more vegetables, I can get two or three *shimlamirch*."

"Yes, yes, but I need a bag of basmati rice. Can't feed a guest coarse boiled rice! And get paneer, and some big chillies, and mustard seeds. And tomatoes, ginger, garlic and fresh coriander. Also, cloves, cardamom, cinnamon. Half a kilo of mutton, half a kilo of chicken. A pinch of *zaffran*. Oh, and carrots for the halwa, and some dry fruits."

There goes the money for the heater, Naina was about to say when she stopped herself.

When was the last time this house had rejoiced in the sound of mustard seeds popping in ladles of ghee? When last had these courtyards swelled with the fragrance of pure basmati flavoured with *zaffran*, and danced to the simmer of a spicy *salan*?

"I'll get the things on my way back in the evening," she said with a smile. "Now I'll go take a bath, and get dressed. I have to leave early today, remember?"

"What is the *gori* going to do over the next few days?" Her aunt asked suspiciously.

"She said she'll be exploring Delhi. She's also going to Rajasthan."

"Rajasthan. Go, go everywhere, see everything," Shakuntala muttered. "Did you give her the directions to this house for Saturday? These *firangs* just need an excuse to get lost."

"We've arranged to meet outside Jantar Mantar," Naina replied, getting up. "I'll give her a brief tour of the old city before bringing her home with me."

"Tour of the old city indeed! Father a tour guide, daughter a tour guide. Father gave away all his wealth, now daughter will give away all hers," Shakuntala said loudly to Naina's retreating back, smacking her lips over the remaining peas.

✦

Today, the class was all energy: students eager to sample new songs, the lilt of the low notes, the passion of the high. They pulled Naina out of her bluish corner, where music and memory always went together, and into a square, laughing patch of light. After the students had left, she locked the harmonium away into the cupboard, deposited the key at the front desk, and walked out of the building. It was a typical December afternoon, cold-reddened faces everywhere, mufflers and monkey caps, the sun dribbling its yellow edges into the sky.

A few yards away from the music school's stone steps, a sleek car waited. Naina was walking towards the main road to flag down her usual bus when the car door opened and a man stepped out. "Hi."

He looked familiar, and Naina smiled in confusion. "Er…hello," she began with sincerity, her expression changing abruptly when she realised it was Varun's friend from the other evening. "Hello," she said again, her eyes wary.

"You remember me. I was thinking you wouldn't…"

"I do. Shekhar. You've come to enroll in music classes?"

"No, no," he replied shyly. "I had gone over to Varun's a couple of times since…since we last met, but you weren't around. So I…came to see you. I learned from Vartika that your classes…"

"To see *me*?" Confusion was giving way to an intense, inexplicable anger. "Why?"

"I…er…wanted to discuss something with you. Look, why don't you get in the car? We can talk on the way," Shekhar replied, holding the door open to his velvet world.

On the front seat sat a uniformed chauffeur, his features impassive, cut in stone.

"You have some nerve," Naina said, raising her voice for the first time for as long as she could remember. "*Get in the car*? No! Please *leave*. Immediately."

Shekhar stared at her, uncomprehending. "I'm sorry," he eventually said, running his hand distractedly through his hair. "I seem to have offended you in some way. Look, please get in, I'll drop you at Varun's. That's where you're headed, isn't it?"

"Yes, for Vartika's music lessons, as you probably know by now. And no, I don't need to be dropped. I'll be taking the bus," Naina threw back, her light green eyes flashing. "And don't you dare come here ever again!"

It was a distracting evening, and Naina found herself staring out of the window more than once. In the garden, the shrubs and bushes huddled close, and beyond the wall, the headlights of cars on the darkening street resembled a hundred fireflies.

"Is everything okay, Didi?" Vartika asked, once the lessons were over.

"Yes," Naina replied absently, gathering her things.

"By the way, did Shekhar-bhai come to see you about his research?"

Naina stared at the younger girl, incredulous. "His *what*?"

"Research," Vartika replied cheerfully. "That's what Shekhar-bhai does. He's very studious. Varun-bhai says he is boring."

"Your Varun-bhai is easily bored," Naina replied dryly. "But listen, I don't understand. What research?"

"Don't know. He says he wants to speak with you, so I give him your number. Then he says he wants to go meet you in person. He's very *proper* that way. He was saying he will take Uncle's car. He sounded so serious it was really funny! Otherwise he travels by buses and trains and stuff."

"But I thought they were rich, like you?"

"Yup. They are. He's weird. I like him. He doesn't tease me like Bhai's other friends," Vartika said, reflecting. "What happened to you?"

"Nothing," Naina said quickly. "I think I might have...never mind. Listen, can you give me your Shekhar-bhai's number?"

✦

That night, after dinner was done and her aunt had gone to bed, Naina dialled Shekhar's number. A ring, two rings, three rings, four, five. They were probably having a party, she mused, the sound of his cellphone drowned in a sea of people loud as waves. She was about to hang up after the sixth ring when he picked up.

"Hullo?"

"Er...hello, is that Shekhar?" All of a sudden, she was wondering if this was a good idea.

"Yes, yes, it is. May I know who...Naina? Is that you?"

"How did you know it's me?" she asked, surprised. "I hope I didn't disturb you..."

"You have a melodious voice, very distinctive. No, you haven't disturbed me at all. I was just sitting and reading. Nothing too important."

"I just called to say.... You know, when you came today...I mean, I'm sorry."

There was silence on the other end. Naina twirled the corner of her dupatta and stood in the shadows, waiting. "That's okay," Shekhar said eventually. "You probably thought I was hitting on you. I should have expressed myself better."

"Vartika said you wanted to speak with me regarding… er…some research? What research? Something on music or dance?"

"No, no, on the old city. I study history at Delhi University, by the way."

"The *old city*? Hmmm. What possible interest could you people from New Delhi have in Old Delhi? And aren't you a little overage for a college student?" Naina asked, regretting her words almost immediately. What was *wrong* with her tongue today? It had never been so loose and unheeding earlier…

"I'm completing my Ph.D," he explained patiently. "It takes several years. Two years for the Masters, two for the M.Phil, three for the doctorate. The good news is that I'm almost done; I'll be defending my dissertation in February."

"I'm sorry," she muttered.

"Don't worry, I didn't mind," he said with sincerity. "So anyway, my doctoral dissertation is on the old city. The industrialisation, the congestion, the cultural erosion. Did you know that when the decision was taken to shift the British capital from Calcutta to New Delhi in 1911, the plan wasn't just to build New Delhi but to also integrate the new city with the old?"

"Really? I didn't know that," she said, surprised. "I had thought New Delhi was basically just a colonial city. That's what my father said."

"No, you're absolutely right. The new city was a consequence of the imperial ambition of severing all connections with the older city ruled by the Mughals. But the initial plan *did* propose a more wholesome integration of the old and the new, and of residential and commercial spaces. Sadly, those roads never got built, and as New Delhi began expanding as a residential and political hub, Shahjahanabad was left to choke on industrial fumes…"

Standing in the dark, Naina nodded. "It was very sad."

"It was more than sad. It was brutal! An elegant old city, once dotted with the havelis, mosques and fountained gardens of a cultured nobility, a city of art and music, now reduced to a chaotic, commercial slum with sixty shops on each lane!"

"Have you visited the old city recently?" she asked, genuinely touched by his passion.

"Of course. Dozens of times. I know that area very well."

"I am really...surprised," she said, at a loss for words.

"When I think of the old city, I think of Ghalib," he continued. "But how many of us would understand the cadence of his couplets today, or even care to?"

His words reminded her of another man, from another time, and his fondness for Ghalib and Faiz. "*Ghalib-e-khasta ke baghair kaun se kaam band hain; Roiye zaar-zaar kya, kijiye hae hae kyun*," she said with a smile.

"*Ham-pesha o ham-mashrab o humraaz hai meraa, Ghalib ko bura kyun kaho achcha mere aage*," he responded. "It's not just Urdu—we have treated so many of our languages so shabbily...we prefer badly-spoken English to well-spoken vernaculars. Globalisation, they call it."

"You're right," she said, a break in her voice. Silence on this side, silence on the other. "So...er...how can I help you?" she finally asked.

"See, I believe oral history can serve as an excellent complement to textual history," he replied earnestly. "I've been interviewing families in the old city for my dissertation, those who've lived there for three generations or more. They were all Muslim, so I have been trying to trace the handful of Hindus in the area. That's how I thought of you."

"Oh, I see. We're not a pure Hindu family though. My great-grandmother was Muslim, and some others before her. Our family has had many Hindu-Muslim marriages."

"How interesting! This will add so much texture to my research. Naina, if you agree, I'd like to interview you along with your family members from older generations. Parents, grandparents..."

"My parents are both dead," Naina said quietly, "and so are my grandparents. I live with my aunt. But sure, the two of us could share our experiences with you."

"I'm sorry to learn of your parents," Shekhar said, his voice gentle. "That must be difficult for you. You must be very brave."

She cradled the phone and smiled. "I don't see myself as brave at all. I fumble, falter, make lots of mistakes..."

"That's true for all of us. But each of today's mistakes makes us that much stronger for tomorrow, does it not?"

"I hope you're right," she said with a sigh. "So will you be giving us a...questionnaire or something?"

"No, no paperwork. We'll just set up a mutually convenient time to meet, and I'll bring a tape recorder. Basically, I want to ask you a few simple questions about your experience of the link between culture and commerce, the old city and the new. The idea is to have a normal, uninterrupted conversation, let people reminisce, say what they really feel."

"I am sure my aunt will love the tape recorder," Naina said, smiling. "It will make her feel very important."

He chuckled. "I am looking forward to meeting her. And...you."

Naina inhaled deeply. "It was nice talking to you, Shekhar. Now I will—"

"Wait, wait, don't hang up," he cut in urgently. "I have something else to ask you. I was wondering if...if we could have lunch together...sometime."

She looked at the trees in the courtyard, naked, their thin arms wrapped around each other. Below them, the fog was touching a trellis with moist fingers and it quivered ever so slightly. From the narrow lane outside came the urgent, shuffling sounds of two dogs. The woman in the house next door hummed an old song, a man whispered in low tones, the woman giggled. Everywhere in nature an intimacy, yet stretched grimly above it all, a wintry, starless sky.

"Naina…? Where are you?"

Where were you? Why didn't I meet you before I met him? She drew in a deep breath. "I don't think lunch is a good idea. You see, I am…"

"That's fine, fine. You don't have to explain, really," he mumbled.

"But I am very interested in your research," she continued gently. "I mean it. Let Vartika know when you want to do the interview, so my aunt and I can be prepared."

Afterwards, undressing and getting into bed, Naina couldn't help thinking about Shekhar's interest in the plight of the old city. And she thought, sleepily, of the white cotton-clad, hazy lines of him, and the lines were slowly coming together, becoming whole, until all of a sudden, Varun's hard body came crashing through, his lips, his laughter everywhere, and all that was left was the darkness swimming all around, and, through the labyrinthine *gali*s of the old city, the distant, unreachable sounds of night.

Excerpts from a Diary

Today he bemoans the impoverishment of the old city, the destruction of a habitat, the death of history. He speaks of its genteel, cultured past, its plentiful promenades, its poetry; then he speaks of the old's neglect at the hands of the new.

If this is now, he asks, can you imagine how it will be twenty, thirty, fifty years from now? Newer cities, with buildings so tall their prices touch the sky, while the older cities and their counter-histories are razed to the ground. A few centres of opulence, and vast numbers of languishing peripheries, soulless, stripped of their past and present, existing only to serve. The very rich and the very poor; that is all we will have.

Ya rab hamen to khvaab mein bhi mat dikhaaiyo, Ye mahshar-e-khayal ki duniya kahe jise...

It is a beautiful day, electric blue sky, carpets of autumn leaves, sunlit alcoves, everywhere the coos of pigeons. They flock together like old women, their grey shawls pulled close to their pointy ears, clucking and gossiping on the cobbled walkway. I really don't want to speak of poverty or prices or counter-histories or culture. Instead, I throw handfuls of seeds in front of the pigeons; their beaks start nudging, their wings are aflutter.

The gap between the rich and the poor has always existed, I point out to him later. I agree that modernisation amplifies this gap, but so what? A people cannot live perpetually in the past; they must modernise, move forward. Modernity is technology, and industries, and airplanes...

And nuclear arsenals and explosives and robots and lonely individuals bereft of community, he counters. Modernity, but at what speed and cost? At the cost of losing all trace of our traditions, having our past entirely obliterated? Colonialism has a vested interest in stripping away our cultural identity, but what when a free country does it to itself, feeds on its own roots? Don't forget that the past is not just that which is ancient and outmoded; in our past also lies our strength, our uniqueness, our eccentricities, our capacity to innovate.

Enough of this glum talk, I declare. Sing the happy, happy songs you always do. I have time; let's go to the gardens. We'll make an early supper of the samosas Amma packed, and you can continue your story about Mriganayani, the tribal girl who became queen of Gwalior. She refused to veil her face in the court, and even fought a few battles alongside her husband—his name was Man Singh Tomar, you said? Or tell me about the courtesans again; theirs is a story I can hear over and over. Tell me how beautiful they were, how talented and ill-fated.

What of the courtesans, he says dubiously. Their stories don't belong to your modern world; they're part of the counter-history that got razed, remember?

Oh, you're impossible today, I say, kicking the stones on the pathway with feeling. I have never seen him sad before. It is I who used to ink blue trails everywhere, till he rose, sun-like, over my horizon, his diamonds rippling through my restless, riverrun days. In my selfish world, there is no place for his sorrow.

Can we have a happy song, please, I ask again, and he finally turns towards me. All right, he says, his fingers drumming a beat on my bare, summer-ripened arm.

A few hours later, after his last song ends, I loop my arm through his. We walk slowly, silently, past the Amaltaas trees at the lip of the Lodhi Gardens, under the light of the falling sun.

Three Women

"Please come," Naina said shyly, holding the door open for Megan. "And be careful—it's a very old house, you know, many uneven edges."

"It's a *beautiful* house." Megan stepped into the courtyard and looked around with interest. "It's like walking into history. Oh, look at those gorgeously carved stairs!"

"It's falling apart," Naina said, a haunting sadness in her eyes. "But we try. We were able to preserve those original stairs. It's a two-storied house, but we only use the ground floor now. Would you like a small tour?"

"Yeah, that will be great," Megan said, handing the bags she was carrying to Naina. "Thanks. Just some things for you and your aunt—fruits, sweets, two shawls."

"Thank you so much. Really very sweet of you. You needn't have gone to so much trouble..."

"It was no trouble at all. The shawls are hand-embroidered, very soft. I hope you like them."

"You couldn't have got us a more thoughtful gift," Naina said with sincerity. "Bua was just complaining the other day that she is tired of her two old shawls." Setting the bags down, she turned to Megan again. "Shall I show you the house now? So this is the courtyard, which we consider a central feature of our homes."

Megan bent down to look more closely at the coloured stones laid out in floral designs. "This is so pretty. From what I've read about courtyards, houses in areas with extreme weather traditionally had these internal open spaces to regulate the temperature, right?"

Naina nodded. "But it's more than just architecture," she said earnestly. "Courtyards are also places for religious rituals and social gatherings, and for children to play. When my parents were alive, we always had something or the other happening here. And after my mother died, my father would sleep here, in the open, under the stars."

"I can imagine. It must be wonderful sleeping here with the cool breeze blowing. And what are those trees?" Megan asked, pointing towards the trees growing inside the compound, their tops expansive, the smaller branches pressed like noses against a broken brick wall.

"That one is a gulmohar. It gets scarlet flowers in April, very vivid. And those other trees are neem. We dry the leaves to use as mosquito repellents, and my aunt also boils them in her drinking water to keep her blood pressure in check. Wonder where she is. Bua, we are here," she called loudly. "Oh, and that tree is jamun, you know, black plums. It will flower around March or April, and the fruits come later in the summer. Children love them very much because they colour the tongue purple. Please come, I'll show you the rooms now."

Naina led the way through the corridor with its classic columns painted with peacock motifs, and into the larger of the two bedrooms. It had pink walls, with ceramic tiles rising half-way from the floors, and a low, gilt painted ceiling. "This is my aunt's bedroom."

"What fascinating architecture and design!"

"Yes. You will not be able to find this kind of design in New Delhi," Naina said with quiet pride. "Especially in the modern houses and apartment complexes they are building nowadays…those are completely westernised."

She guided Megan further down the corridor, to her own bedroom. This room was much smaller, the paint peeling off its walls in many places. But Megan admired the small touches, like the printed cotton bedspread and the jute carpet at the foot of the bed. She was also enthralled by the carved wooden door opening into the veranda, as she was by the stone latticework. "Did you plant these?" she asked Naina, pointing to the creepers growing out of small earthen pots. "And where did you buy these lovely painted pots?"

"I painted those."

"Wait, you mean you painted them yourself?" Megan ran the tip of her index finger over the intricate design on one of them. "They're *awesome*!"

"Thanks. Just simple poster paints," Naina said, embarrassed.

"No, I mean it. You're very talented." Megan walked out of the room and back into the corridor. "Are we going upstairs too?" she asked, looking at the wooden stairs.

"Er…there is really nothing much to see upstairs," Naina replied after some hesitation. "There were two more rooms and a large veranda, but it's all crumbling and cordoned off now…"

"No problem at all," Megan said, her eyes drawn to a framed wall photograph of a dancer in traditional costume. "Hey, look at that. Is that you?"

Naina nodded. "I dance…*used to* dance Kathak. That's from a stage performance a few years ago."

"Kathak?" Megan walked up to the photograph to admire Naina's graceful posture and her elaborate costume. "I haven't heard of it, but I'll google it tonight."

"It's one of India's classical dances. There are many different schools of Kathak—we call them 'gharana'. I trained in the Lucknow gharana."

"And what are those things you are wearing around your ankles? Is that part of the costume?"

"Yes, those are called *ghungroos*. Anklets, but heavier than normal ones. See those tiny bells all around? They make a beautiful musical sound."

"Fascinating. And are you dancing to recorded music here, or live?"

"Here it's a recording, but traditionally, it was live. The vocal composition was considered as important as the dance composition, you see. In this gharana, we dance either to Indian semi-classical musical forms like thumri, or lighter forms like *dadra, hori, kajari*. The stylisation...oh no!"

The house had plunged into complete darkness. "What's happened?" Megan's voice rang out in the dark.

"It's the electricity. Goes off anytime, day or night," Naina replied apologetically. "Now it won't be back for at least an hour. We will have to light some candles."

Just then, the sound of footsteps, a drawer being pulled, a flickering light from the corridor. "Naina, *kahan ho tum log*?"

"Bua," Naina called out loudly. Then, lowering her voice, "My aunt. She must have been taking a bath. She never does that in the evening, that too in winter. I think it's because you were coming tonight..."

"Seems she's got a candle. Shall we go out?"

"No, no, you might trip in the dark. Please wait here. I'll go light more candles, and bring Bua."

Shakuntala pulled out another drawer, the candle in her hand tilting precariously and dribbling wax onto Naina's outstretched palm.

"Ow!! Bua!"

"Is everything Bua's fault? You should have invited her for lunch; at least we would have had sunlight. No, Bua, let us invite her for dinner, dinner! I hope the members of the electricity board get diarrhoea. Tapeworm, ringworm, hope their bowels burst!"

"Stop cursing and give me that candle. You'll burn me to death."

"Death, she talks of death," Shakuntala grumbled, handing her niece the candle and lighting a second one. "Do you know what death is? Do you know how much—"

"Okay, okay," Naina interrupted hastily, pulling at the sleeve of her aunt's kameez. "Let's go. Megan is waiting inside."

They walked down the corridor, shielding the candle flames with the palms of their hands. "There she is. Megan, meet my aunt," Naina said. "And Bua, this is Megan."

✦

Shakuntala lifted the candle to Megan's face and drew back with a gasp. The girl's eyes, her lips! A heavy mist rolled in through the open courtyard, and Shakuntala shivered.

"Hullo, so pleased to meet you. You have a lovely home," Megan was saying, coming forward to give the older woman a hug.

Hullo, so pleased to meet you. You have a lovely home. It was summer again, green, everything green, with tall flowers, and in their midst, a girl washed with colour. Afterwards, the sun so black and stinging, and the same flowers, dead and dry like paper. Shakuntala's heart rattled against her ribs. "Dinner. Ready," she said in English to Naina, walking out of the room on wooden legs.

"Your aunt is very quiet. An introvert," Megan remarked to Naina.

Naina giggled. "I wish our neighbours could hear you say that. Bua's morning begins with shouting at the vegetable seller and the street dogs, and ends with shouting at the people next door, the members of the electricity board, the President of the country! No, I think it's the language barrier. She understands some English, but she's obviously not very comfortable. Plus she doesn't know you…"

"I understand." Megan followed Naina through the corridor and into the kitchen, where Naina's aunt had lit four sturdy candles. "My God, it smells *good* in here," she said, sniffing appreciatively. "Did your aunt cook everything herself?"

"Yes, she is a tremendous cook. And she has a good heart. I don't know what I would have done without her."

Megan was looking at all the food arranged on the floor, in copper containers and cast-iron cooking pots, and the mats spread out in a circle around it. "Do you guys eat here, on the kitchen floor?" she asked, curious.

"We do in this house. My parents, and their parents before them, found the idea of eating at a dining table too westernised. That tradition has continued. I can pull up a chair for you if you like."

"No worries. This is all so interesting for me," Megan said, lowering herself and sitting cross-legged, like Naina. "Should I just help myself?" she asked, reaching out for the ladle.

"No, no, Bua will be *most* offended if you do. We serve our guests ourselves," Naina said, smiling at her aunt who had just shuffled in behind them.

"Nawabi biryani, *mirch ka salan, kastoori kabab, shimlamirch bharwain,* raita," Shakuntala pronounced with satisfaction, lifting the lids off the containers one by one. "And *gajar ka halwa.*"

The aroma was tantalising, and Megan's stomach rumbled. "Now you know my stomach's feelings on the subject. But really, you needn't have cooked so many things," she said, quite overwhelmed. "Thank you *so* much. I know biryani, but not this specific one. And I've never heard of the other stuff. Naina, would you please translate for me?"

"Yes, yes, of course. Nawabi biryani is like mutton biryani, very famous in Lucknow. The kebabs are made of chicken, rolled in an egg-and-gramflour batter with lots of spices. The *salan* is just chillies—see these fat green ones? Cooked in a gravy of peanuts and coconut. And *shimlamirch* is—"

"Green pepper?"

"Oh, we say capsicum. Bua has stuffed it with paneer – cottage cheese, that is – and the raita is just a yogurt…dip, an accompaniment. And the dessert, *gajar ka halwa*, is made of grated carrot, with…"

"Oh, carrot fudge!" Megan cut in triumphantly. "This I've eaten in the US!"

"That's what you call it there? Carrot fudge?" Naina asked, smiling.

Shakuntala scooped biryani out of the pressure cooker and raised her eyebrow at Megan, who obediently held up her plate. After ladling generous portions of all the other dishes onto her plate, Shakuntala served Naina and herself. "How?" she asked Megan.

"*Fantastic*," Megan replied enthusiastically, after she'd tasted everything. "Naina was right—you really are a great cook!"

Shakuntala beamed. "You call me Bua," she said, in the manner of a queen bestowing a huge favour, and glared at Naina, who had started giggling. "Why laugh?" she asked her niece in English, bringing forth another spurt of giggles. "Silly," Shakuntala said crossly, before digging into her own food.

"My Rajasthan trip was excellent," Megan said, turning to smile at Naina, who was still giggling. "It was just for a couple of days, so I could only go to Jaipur and Udaipur, but everything I saw was breathtaking. Have you been there?"

Naina nodded. "As a child. When both my parents were alive," she said softly. "I must have been seven or eight. I remember a camel ride, and maybe a little bit of the Hawa Mahal."

"Oh, the Hawa Mahal was incredible! Its layout, architecture, the women's chambers… I could almost imagine the royal women from the 1800s sitting behind those window screens in *purdah* and watching the world go by. And you know what? I said something about the chill winds that were constantly blowing, and then the guide told me that Hawa Mahal means the Palace of Winds!"

"That's right. My parents also told me about a puppet show they had taken me to see, but I don't remember that at all," Naina said, the sadness back in her eyes. "Did you see any puppet shows?"

"No, but I did see a traditional dance, you know, the one where they twirl around in those long, colourful skirts? Afterwards, I bought one of those skirts from a nearby bazar. It's embroidered, with lots of mirrors, very pretty."

"The skirt is called a *ghagara*." Naina helped herself to more biryani. "And the dance is called Ghoomar."

"Yeah, that's what it was. Speaking of which, when will I be able to see you dance, Naina?"

"Yes, tell, tell," Shakuntala suddenly shouted, almost making Megan drop her plate.

Naina drew in a long breath. "I don't dance anymore, Megan," she said quietly. "I don't know how to explain…"

"Hey, you don't *have* to," Megan said, taking Naina's hand impulsively. "Maybe you just don't feel like dancing anymore. That's a good enough explanation for me!"

Naina looked at Megan gratefully. "Bua doesn't always understand…"

"No, Bua understand everything," Shakuntala snapped. "Bua not understand English? Bua understand, understand. Bua ask, Bua tell."

The two young women looked at Shakuntala in surprise. *Well then*, Megan thought. *Why all the subterfuge? Why don't you come straight out and tell me?*

Shakuntala had gone back to gnawing the meat off a succulent piece of chicken. "More?" she asked Megan with her mouth full.

"Thank you, Bua. This was the nicest dinner I have had in a long, long time, but no more food," Megan replied, suddenly resolute. "I want something else from you. Tell me this—where is Karim Street? And...Naina, what happened? Are you okay?"

Naina had started choking on her last morsel of biryani, and her aunt began to thwack her on her back. When Naina's spluttering had subsided, Shakuntala turned to Megan with an expression of pure victory. "Karim Street," she said, her eyes glazing. "In Lucknow. Long time ago."

✦

"So...you mean this street was famous for a *brothel*?" Megan asked slowly. From what she had been able to piece together of Shakuntala's broken phrases, delivered while aunt and niece were putting away the leftover food, that is what it appeared. "The women of Karim Street were prostitutes? Sex workers?"

This time it was Shakuntala's turn to splutter. Wiping her hands on her dupatta, she launched into a diatribe in her own language, the words shooting out of her mouth like poisoned arrows.

"What is Bua saying?" Megan asked, uncomprehending. "Naina...?"

"Bua is saying they – the women, that is – were not *randis*, common prostitutes," Naina replied quietly. "They were *tawaifs*, courtesans."

"Huh? And the difference is?"

"See, common prostitutes only provide sexual services. But the courtesans...that was an era, an entire culture of grace, elegance, of rigorous education even," Naina replied earnestly.

"Education?"

"Yes. A courtesan would receive *years* of training in literature, etiquette, dance and music before she was allowed to make her first public appearance. Courtesans have played quite a huge role in enriching our country's traditions in music and art, you know. And sexuality—that too was considered an art, an ancient art..."

"You mean, like in the *Kamasutra*?"

"Yes," Naina replied, colouring slightly. "The courtesans of Lucknow were formally trained in the art of...of lovemaking. See, you had to be really beautiful *and* talented in order to be a courtesan. Bua says a courtesan would earn at least twenty times the amount earned by a common prostitute for a single night...and she would also receive other lavish gifts, like jewellery, and property, political positions even."

"Wow," Megan said, eyes widening. "But tell me, who were these women to *begin* with? Obviously, they must have been orphans or destitute or discarded by their families for some other reason, right? I mean, otherwise why would they want to take up what must have been considered a shameful profession like this..."

"No," Shakuntala yelled, the veins on her temples angry and swollen like rain-fed rivers. "No, no, shame, no!"

"Bua, blood pressure," Naina interrupted, worried. "What you are saying may be true," she continued, turning to Megan, "and many of the women may already have been social outcasts before they entered the *kotha*. But a few, I believe, had voluntarily left their households to experience the *kotha*'s freedom. Because the *kotha*s were very – how shall I put it – women-centred."

"Really? How do you mean?"

"Because men were in subordinate roles," Naina explained. "As musicians and accompanists."

"And what about pimps?"

"Hmm. I don't know if pimps were all that common back then. Maybe."

"And who ran the *kotha*?"

"There wasn't so much hierarchy, I think. The head was the *chaudhrayan*, an older, retired courtesan who looked after the girls' welfare. Finances were in the hands of the women, as was the decision of which patrons to entertain and whom to throw out."

"They must all have had to provide sexual services though?"

"I'm not sure about that. I think some of them could choose to just be performers. Singers and dancers, that is. But see, the important thing is that sex was, was not..."

"Something to be ashamed of?" Megan offered helpfully. "Female sexuality was something to be celebrated, unlike the larger society. That's what you're trying to say, right?"

"Exactly."

"Very interesting. Tell me more."

"Well, it's a long story...why don't I light a fire first?" Naina asked.

"You have a fireplace?"

"No, we just light a fire outside, in a little space we cleared out at the edge of the courtyard. It's cold, I know, but you must be used to much colder weather? Otherwise we can take some candles inside, to my room."

"The fire sounds good," Megan said, rubbing her palms together. "You go light the fire, and I will make some tea for all of us."

"No, no," Naina exclaimed, perturbed. "We don't let guests do any work. Please be comfortable. I'll make the tea."

"But I'm American, remember? I'm just not used to being waited upon! Let me do something, please."

"All right. We don't have teabags though," Naina laughed. "You'll have to boil the water with the tea leaves, milk and sugar, and then strain it into cups."

"Boil it *with* the milk and sugar?" Megan asked, intrigued. "Okay, show me where everything is, let me try. Maybe a really good cup of tea will help me get back into Bua's good books again."

By the time Megan came into the courtyard, balancing three steaming mugs of tea on a tray, Naina was throwing bunches of dried twigs into a fire. Shakuntala wore a striped woollen scarf and sat on a cot, her stubby legs dangling over its edge like washing on a clothesline. She looked less miffed than earlier, but wouldn't look at Megan.

"See, I made tea for you, Bua," Megan said softly. "Here, take this one; it has more milk. Naina, you can take the other one."

Naina nursed the mug in her palms before taking a sip. "This is perfect, Megan."

"No. No perfect," said Shakuntala stubbornly, rocking her legs when the girls laughed.

"And now will you continue with the story?" Megan asked hopefully.

"It's more Bua's story to tell. Whatever I know, I have heard from her," Naina replied, turning to her aunt. "If she agrees to tell it, I can translate for you. Bua?"

Shakuntala grunted and looked away.

"Please Bua," Naina said gently. "See, Megan has come all the way from America. She is our guest…"

"Please Bua," Megan said, clapping her hands in glee when Shakuntala nodded.

"What?" Shakuntala asked, turning to Megan.

"Tell Bua what you want to know," Naina prompted.

You know perfectly well what I want to know, Bua. But if you insist on telling other stories, I will play along with you. Aloud, Megan said, "Well then, tell me about the courtesans of Karim Street."

Shakuntala cleared her throat, took a deep breath, and began. The fire in the courtyard was blazing and dots of bright light danced on her face. All around them was the night, moonless, wrapped in mists, magically transporting Megan to another time and place. As Shakuntala, carried away by her tale, let go of all inhibition and Naina, looking a little embarrassed, started translating swiftly, Megan could almost hear the perfumed giggles of the courtesans and the silvered sounds of their anklets.

Slowly, Shakuntala's simple words and Naina's sweet voice began to recede into the background and another voice seemed to take over, the voice of history, omniscient and evocative.

The Courtesans of Karim Street

The culture of courtesans is as ancient as the blood that runs through the swollen arteries of history. While angry processions marched down city streets in the blaze of sun, armed with paperbacks and pamphlets on women's freedom, the boulevards of those same cities were perfumed by the night musk of women who had always been free. Often of lowly birth, they paved their way through the labyrinthine world of power and pelf with their silvery, seductive laughter, the fragrant cleft between their breasts, and their wet, wise ministrations that left kings and courtiers kindled and quivering.

These were pragmatic times, when marriages were contracted to secure dwindling political fortunes and to preserve the bloodline, and wives undressed in stiff, mute preparation for their nightly bludgeoning. After the husbands had rolled off and staggered drunkenly back to their own quarters, these women thanked their stars and hoped for good news. And when the visits grew more and more infrequent, especially after male heirs were born, the wives dared not complain of this callousness, let alone refuse their masters; no, the right of refusal belonged only to the courtesan.

When the courtesan sought or welcomed union, her limbs were supple and yielding, her breath as soft and stealthy as the moonflower night. But when she refused, her eyes burnt holes into the hardened hearts of her suitors and they hung their heads. But how is this possible, you ask. Well, you see, once a courtesan's fame had soared like the wings of the eagle, many skies were open to her. Determined to outbid their fellowmen, nobles vying for her favours came to her door with not just gifts of jewels, carriages, fine silks and aged wines, but with tempting invitations to inner circles of royalty and privilege. Such was the power wielded by a well-received courtesan, and the men who had been lucky to be bestowed with her companionship paid for it with money and meekness. In return, the courtesan used her warm mouth, tiny nibbles of her teeth, the pointy tip of her tongue, her splayed feet and the soft trail of her hair to bring her men a pleasure so exquisite that, decades later, their wasted bodies would tingle and rise with the memory.

Yet beautiful bodies were not the only gifts the courtesans had to offer; no, more priceless were the gifts of dance, music and poetry. These were talented women, with rigorous training in the arts; a few of them even went down in the pages of history as poetesses and performers of renown. As priceless was their wit; and more so, their wisdom, for they held considerable knowledge of politics, and used it freely for their own, and their men's, welfare. Weary of court intrigues, men walked into the courtesans' flowery, fountained abode to find not just sensuality and indulgence but also information and intelligent advice. The courtesans could be kingmakers, and the fates of many kingdoms lay sealed in the space between their legs.

Of course, every once in a while, a courtesan became the custodian of so many prized secrets that her life needed to be ended on the same precise note on which it had begun; in these instances, poisoning was the preferred mode, though one does occasionally hear of kings with a penchant for public beheadings. These over-enthusiastic displays aside, more common were snake venom, the blood of lizards and leeches, and later, arsenic. Anything that could come unnoticed, in the stillness of night, for death, in high circles, must be discreet.

More often, though, a courtesan made a more lethal lapse, not of revealing political secrets to those that held keys to larger coffers, but, quite simply, of falling in love. These courtesans who forgot the fundamental rule of their mothers' and grandmothers' trades, and used their hearts rather than their heads, paid for it a price dearer than death. But more of that later.

For now, you must be curious to know about the courtesans of Karim Street.

✦

When Rukhsana Jan was born in Lucknow in 1858 – no one knows the exact month and date, but some say it was a rainy night, and that the same night a thunderbolt struck the city, and an ancient tree collapsed with a resounding groan, and a pandit and a maulvi died under its branches in the middle of a heated argument – the courtesans of Lucknow were still a force to reckon with.

Lucknow, situated three hundred miles southeast of Delhi, was, as you probably know, the capital of the Muslim kingdom of Awadh from 1775 till 1856. It remained a seat of power under the imperial government from 1856 to 1947, and is now the capital of the state of Uttar Pradesh in independent India. Well, so the courtesans of Lucknow had flourished under the patronage of not just the merchants and other elite groups of the city but also the king of Awadh Nawab Wajid Ali Shah himself, who maintained a large harem of courtesans by using a variant of Islamic marriage called *mutah*, entering into numerous marriage contracts that expired after a stipulated time. He married both Hindu and Muslim courtesans, gifting them some of Lucknow's best real estate which allowed them to hone their arts undisturbed. Having enthralled the city with their *nakhra* and their *nazakat* for decades, having manipulated scores of nawabs for political privileges and driven scores of others to lovesickness and financial ruin, these 'nautch girls', as they were disparagingly called by the British administration, had even sung and danced their way into the civic tax ledgers as taxpayers, making them not just the only women to figure in the imperial tax records at all, but also to find pride of place in the highest tax brackets, among the richest individuals in the city.

In 1856, Awadh was annexed by the British, the royal court disbanded, and Nawab Wajid Ali Shah dethroned and exiled. In 1857, the first war of Indian independence burned its way through Lucknow and the rest of India. What had begun as a small act of rebellion by the soldier Mangal Pandey was taken up by scores of other Indian soldiers; soon, peasants groaning under imperial tax regimes had joined in the mutiny, as had disposed kings and nawabs from Delhi to the Deccan. The flickering light of independence was rapidly turning into a conflagration, and conches were being blown in anticipation of an Indian victory. As is the nature of such things, however, the imperial administration soon killed the mutiny as well as the mutineers, tying them to the mouths of canons and blowing them up into bloody bits of flesh and limbs, and soon afterwards, control of India was transferred from the East India Company to the British Crown. Many sweeping changes followed, in order to ensure that revolts did not reoccur and British rule over the Indian subcontinent could carry on uninterrupted for the next century. As for the courtesans, many of them had their taxes doubled and their *kotha*s, cashboxes, and mango orchards confiscated by the imperial administration for providing shelter to the rebels during the revolt.

The doubling of taxes and the stripping away of a sturdy capital base was hardly good news for business, and the *ittar* in the small jewelled decanters lining the shelves of the *kotha*s began to dry up, the rows of unlit lamps in the garden hid their faces like rusticated schoolboys, and the courtesans took to bed with unidentified ailments, penning *nazm a*fter throbbing *nazm* on death and devastation instead of love, lust and liberty.

On Karim Street too, the mood was sombre, and anyone who heard that not a single patron had swished in through the sequined curtains hanging at the fountained entrance of this *kotha* for almost a year immediately died in disbelief. For, you see, the *kotha* on Karim Street was the king of *kotha*s, its courtesans the most renowned in all of Lucknow. These courtesans had skin the colour of molten butter, eyes as green as clear-cut emeralds, cheeks whose blush reduced roses to withering agony, and lips like the hungry swell of monsoon. When they sang raga Malhar, the heavens parted and silvery showers poured forth; when they danced, their blazing *ghungroo*s scorched a trail through the papery hearts of men. If they be men of means, they flocked to the *kotha* with gifts of rubies and sapphires, and if they be poor, they sat all night on the hard pavement outside the metal gates of the *kotha*, where morning discovered them frozen in death, a smile on their lips to indicate they had reached *jannat*.

So obviously, the dwindling business on Karim Street was enough to flabbergast even the most dispassionate of onlookers. If this can happen to the courtesans of Karim Street, they declared with a resolute shake of their heads, the glorious days of Lucknow are over, over. Why, last year, the *kotha* had been forced to let go of the dozens of part-time help who had come and gone through those gates for years, bringing trinkets, tailored blouses, medicines, milk and vegetables, fresh fish just arrived from the east and a dozen other things...the errand boys, the palanquin bearers, the *maalishwali* with her bottles of herbal oil that she rubbed on the aching feet of the older courtesans, the cobbler who came each Tuesday to mend their leather *jooti*s, the silversmith who polished their hookahs every second week, had all had their outstanding dues cleared and been asked not to return for a year.

Only a handful of the most faithful servants who had served the *kotha* for generations were retained to do the groceries, the cooking, and the repairs; these minions operated silently, through side doors that opened out onto narrow bylanes stained with paan-juices and puddles. As for the rest, the gates of the *kotha*s were padlocked from inside with thick heavy chains. Summer turned to autumn, and autumn to winter, as passers-by sniffled and dabbed their eyes at the desolate sight of the *kotha*, now hidden under an untidy overgrowth of shrubs and vines.

These passers-by would have been very surprised indeed, had they known of the absolute frenzy inside the *kotha* even as it remained dead to the outside world. For the courtesans, you see, were engaged in the impossible task of trying to teach a soldier how to play a *sarangi*.

✦

The story was this: a rebel soldier being chased down Chowk Bazaar by a contingent of British soldiers had scaled the walls of the *kotha* on Karim Street at midnight to find himself in the sleeping chambers of a certain young courtesan with enchanting eyes. This rebel soldier had been one of the frontrunners in the siege of Lucknow, and they said he, along with the other rebels, had fired muskets into the compound of the residency of the British High Commissioner and later dug an underground tunnel into the compound that had led to close combat with the East India Company's sepoys. The combat had lasted for almost three months and resulted in the death of hundreds of British soldiers as well as the Commissioner himself. However, soon afterwards, an imperial army led by a new commander-in-chief had marched into Lucknow; fresh from a victory over the rebellion in Kanpur, the army had succeeded in driving the brave but disorganised rebels from Awadh, killing and maiming as many of the rebels they could, and putting a price on the heads of those they couldn't.

Well, so this particular soldier trying to escape the bullets of the British battalion suddenly found himself staring into a pair of enchanting eyes, and dropped his gun in confusion. And the enchanting eyes, having been roused from sleep by a slithering sound on the walls, saw a tall, handsome man whose moustache curled like the scorpion's tail. What else can be said but that two milky-white arms beckoned, two staggering, bullet-riddled legs led, and a scarlet kiss was planted upon a dusty forehead.

Rumour has it that they remained in bed for sixty days and sixty nights, and that by the time word of this state of affairs reached the *chaudharayan* of the *kotha*, a dizzy spell, a high-pitched demand for sour pickle, and the sounds of morning sickness had made turning the rebel over to his death at the hands of the British Commander-in-Chief quite out of the question. It wasn't just a matter of patriotism, even less about an illicit birth, for the courtesans had always had a pragmatic approach to both politics and pregnancy. No, it was about *love*, the lethal weapon that had killed many a courtesan before, and would kill again, if something were not done immediately. For it was known in every lane of Lucknow that the courtesans of Karim Street only loved once. She loved him; if he died, she would too, and that could not be allowed to happen. So, while the flat river belly of the young courtesan began to swell tidally, the *kotha* was closed off to the public and all attention diverted towards the task of teaching the soldier the subtle nuances of ragas Bihaag and Baghesree.

There is no solid proof to back this claim, of course, but some say that when the *kotha* reopened its doors a year later – after many of its cashboxes had been confiscated by the British, via an imperial order passed on through the side-door, for you see, treason was suspected though it never could be confirmed – there was a certain *sarangi* player whose instrument seemed just a little out of tune, and who gripped this delicate instrument with steely, grim-lipped resolve, almost like one would a bayonet.

Regardless of what you choose to believe, the one fact you cannot dispute is this: in 1858, a young girl was born in that *kotha* on Karim Street, and she would go on to become the famous Rukhsana Jan.

✦

By the time the *kotha* on Karim Street unlocked its rusted gates again, about a year from the date on which they had been padlocked, the city's salon culture had suffered huge setbacks. The patronage of Wajid Ali Shah and his chief courtiers had ended following his exile, and huge fines been imposed on *kotha*s by the imperial administration; direr though, was the added burden of legal regulations. European soldiers had begun to be diagnosed with venereal diseases, you see, and after some of them died, the Indian equivalent of the British Contagious Diseases Act came into force. This Act required the regular medical examination of prostitutes and their constant monitoring by the administration, a requirement that was as sternly enforced as the requirement that the most beautiful of these courtesans make themselves available for unpaid sex with European officers and their soldiers in the cantonments.

This British policy of officially maligning the courtesans while unofficially using their bodies as perks for the imperial administration resulted in the slow descent of an age-old cultural institution into common prostitution. Many *kotha*s perished completely. But not so the *kotha* on Karim Street. For, despite a hundred hurdles, the courtesans of Karim Street remained the best in the business, combining talent with tactics of subtle subterfuge, beauty with bribery and blackmail, to continue to thrive and consolidate themselves. In a few years, the *kotha* had not just re-established itself financially, but also adapted to the musical tastes of their new patrons—the *taluqdars* of Awadh, a powerful rural class which was fast transforming into the city's urban elite. Now you could hear the silvery strains of thumri and ghazal all day long, as the courtesans cleared their throats for *riyaaz* at sunrise and put away the tanpura only at sunset. And so, the *kotha* on Karim Street had already developed a solid reputation in Hindustani semi-classical music by the time Rukhsana came of age.

Of Rukhsana's beauty, it is said that the sun would sit sulking inside grey bowls of cloud until she, of the emerald eyes and rosebud lips, walked to her window and smiled; then, sunrise, the liquid spill of russet colours across a half-crazed sky. It is also said that the moon waxed when Rukhsana untied her robe and stepped, long-limbed and high-breasted, into a scented bath, and waned after she'd shimmered out of water and tied her robe back on again. As her beauty, so her talent; as a young girl, Rukhsana showed a remarkable interest in Urdu poetry and Hindustani music, and by sixteen, was composing and singing ghazals of her own. In the mornings, she sailed through the garden like a mist, streams of songs coursing unbidden through her summer-ripened body; in the evening, she sat on the stone steps of the courtyard, dipping her quill in flaming red ink to pen them down. She wrote mostly of love and longing, and when these scraps of paper found their way to the *kotha*'s aging, bolster-propped *chaudhrayan*, the latter took long, satisfied drags from her hookah.

Two years later, on the evening of her first *mujra*, Rukhsana wore a flowing, pearl-encrusted *sharara*, with glittering emerald jewellery to match the tone of her eyes. Her long tresses had been perfumed with sandalwood incense, and her smooth white skin had been rubbed with a paste of milk and turmeric until it glowed. The evening lamps were lit, patrons welcomed with platters of paan and sprinkles of *ittar*, and then the usual chatter, naughty and boisterous. Then Rukhsana entered on a beam of moonlight, and a hush descended upon the gathering; she lifted her veil, and the audience gasped at this vision of unearthly beauty. And when she started singing, her heaving breasts in rhythm with her dulcet voice, a hundred hearts tumbled onto the floor like small change.

Within the week, gossip in the bazar had established Rukhsana Jan as the *most* beautiful and the *most* talented of the courtesans of Karim Street. Her heart became a prize that Lucknow's rich and powerful men sought at the cost of losing everything they had—wife, children, mistresses, bungalows, fruit orchards, and family heirlooms. The *kotha* on Karim Street had entered the most glorious period of its life.

✦

So, did Rukhsana Jan fall in love? What we know for sure is that, even though she had a dozen and more proposals from kings and courtiers, poets and politicians, even European officers of the highest rank, she never married. And while it was common among courtesans to say no to marriage – and some say it was because these women enjoyed more freedom and independence as courtesans than they could ever hope to, as subservient wives in male-centric households – rumour has it that Rukhsana Jan did, in fact, wish to marry.

The man in question was a Hindu prince named Roshan, who had visited the *kotha* at the insistence of his friends. During Rukhsana's performance, his fingers had drummed the *teentaala* beat along with the tabla, his head tilting to her notes, his eyes closed in rapture rather than gaping at Rukhsana's beauty as other men in the gathering were wont to do. Afterwards, Rukhsana saw him earnestly trying to explain the intricacies of taal and *laya* to his drunken, brawling friends. When he was leaving after making a more than suitable offering to the *chaudhrayan*, Rukhsana happened to trip ever so slightly on a curling corner of the silk *dari*; rushing to her side, he steadied her, his tall, dark, sherwani-clad form complementing her softer, more ethereal frame. And in the split second when her bodice shifted and the sequined *chunri* slid off her shoulders to reveal the high spill of her milky breasts, and all the men present in the room leaned in for a closer look, he gently re-arranged the shimmering garment over her bodice before lowering his eyes respectfully.

Instead of saying "*khuda-hafiz*" and walking away, she stood transfixed. Feeling her continued gaze upon him, he looked up in confusion; their eyes met, and held, and her musk mingled with his heat.

That night, Rukhsana was twenty-two and Roshan twenty-five. That night, neither was able to sleep for a long time, he in his royal palace and she on her balcony under the stars, and when they did, each dreamt of the other's touch. Waking at dawn's rouse, their flesh searing, they knew their fates had been sealed by Kaamadeva, the lord of love. According to bazar gossip, they met regularly after that, continuing even after marriage was ruled out – his illustrious family would have none of it, and his mother took ill and refused to recover until he'd consented to marry the daughter of the wealthiest Hindu merchant in the city – and, for the next twenty years, it was Roshan that Rukhsana always thought of whenever anyone mentioned the word 'husband.' As for falling in love with another man, that very possibility had ceased to be from the moment her emerald eyes had met his amber ones. Yes, you have guessed the reason—the courtesans of Karim Street only loved once.

And so it would have continued till the end of time, this unspoken marriage between an elegant woman and an honour-bound man, had the man not been diagnosed with a rare illness by the royal physician and given only a few months to live. It was the year 1900, and Rukhsana Jan was forty-one. Her parents had died twelve years ago – her ex-soldier father had, after thirty years of hiding, been found and publicly hanged by the imperial administration, and her mother had swallowed her diamond ring when she heard the news. Now, with the news of Roshan's impending death, Rukhsana felt orphaned all over again. That is when she decided to have a baby. Believe it or not, it was then that the elegant woman and the honour-bound man chose, for the very first time, to step out of the bounds of elegance and honour to consummate their 'marriage.' And call it a miracle of nature, call it God's justice after a long, long trial, call it what you will, but Rukhsana Jan conceived. In the year 1901, a beautiful little girl was born with the trademark green eyes of Karim Street. Rukhsana named her daughter Roshanara, in the memory of the recently-dead Roshan.

✦

Roshanara's story is simpler. She grew up to be almost as beautiful and talented as her mother, and had been performing at the *kotha* for nearly seven years when she fell in love with a Hindu merchant travelling to Lucknow on business. Courtesans usually stopped performing by the age of thirty, maybe thirty-five, and the twenty-five year-old Roshanara had already begun to worry about her retirement and a solitary, sad future. Bearing witness to her mother's tragic life, defined as much by the presence of untold luxuries as by the absence of an unnamed lover, had turned Roshanara into something of a rebel; she wanted to marry, and to have legitimate children. So when the merchant asked her to marry him, she agreed, and the two decided to elope.

The women of the bazar say that, inner agitations notwithstanding, the petite, pliable Roshanara lacked the will to execute something as daring as this, and that the elopement had the blessing of the formidable Rukhsana Jan herself. It was Rukhsana Jan, now in her sixties and the *chaudhrayan* of the *kotha*, who heard her daughter babbling in a heat of hope – *if he goes away and marries another, I will become a living corpse* – and resolved that her daughter's fate would be different from her own. Summoning the merchant in the stealth of night, she asked him his intentions, and upon being convinced that he truly intended to marry Roshanara, Rukhsana Jan asked them to leave Lucknow before dawn. She also gifted Roshanara her prized *potli* of jewels – the famous emerald necklace and *jhumka*s that had been handed down generations of women on Karim Street, a diamond tiara, a topaz ring, a sapphire pendant, several gold bangles, and a pair of heavy silver anklets that she had worn many decades ago, on that sultry evening when she first met her prince Roshan.

So it was in the year 1926 that Roshanara, daughter of the fabled Rukhsana Jan, left her foremothers' home in Lucknow and came to Delhi, where her new husband's forefathers had bequeathed on him a haveli. Positioned at an unseemly angle on a narrow side street, it was much too rambling a house for just the two of them. But to Roshanara, this was home, and she swept and mopped its floors endlessly, set up her kitchen with its gleaming rows of pots and pans, sewed curtains and matching bedspreads, and hung up bunches of green chillies at the doorway to ward off evil spirits.

This was the house where Roshanara was formally re-christened Roshni, though some say she remained Muslim within the privacy of their home, reading her namaz five times a day while her Hindu husband knelt in front of the goddess Lakshmi's golden idol. Some also say that when her husband's dwindling income could no longer support their household and he suggested they sell the jewels that Rukhsana Jan had given to her daughter as a wedding gift, Roshni refused; instead, she discreetly began to ply her ancient trade once again, and made a slapping success of it. And with this, the courtesans of Lucknow's Karim Street had now imprinted themselves on the country's capital city, so much so that the side-street on which Roshni and her husband's haveli was located began to be referred to as Karim Street among a select set.

Is it true that Roshni lost her first baby in the middle of a high energy *chakkar*, during one of her Kathak performances for her patrons? Well, who knows! The good news was that, some years later, she did conceive again. In 1931, the year the first British viceroy entered the newly built Viceregal Lodge atop Raisina Hill and New Delhi as the seat of national government was formally inaugurated, a beautiful, green-eyed girl was born in the old city.

✦

Now, very few people remember this girl's real name because her parents called her many different names to suit their own changing moods. This girl learnt much from her mother, like how to make her singing voice dulcet with warm honey, how to perform the most complex of Kathak *tukda*s, how to sway like a lily in the breeze, how to deftly prepare paan with areca nuts, cloves, cardamoms and rose petals, how to make a man feel like one. But there was something she didn't learn from anyone, something that was entirely her own, and this was her habit of saying *Ya Allah Hey Bhagwan*. Visitors to their house were often impressed by how remarkably secular she was, how she always invoked Hindu as well as Muslim gods. But this girl was merely pragmatic; she liked to keep all her bases covered.

This girl turned sixteen in August 1947, her birthday coinciding with the month and year of India's freedom from British rule, and even though the newly independent state had declared prostitution in any and every form to be an offence against women and therefore illegal, some say that she too discreetly carried on her family's courtesan tradition and some say she did not.

This girl married an impoverished, idealistic musician who moved into their haveli soon after the nuptials, and while this arrangement may seem peculiar to more patriarchal mindsets, we must remember that in courtesan culture, it was common for girls to inherit what their mothers and grandmothers owned, and for men to be quite irrelevant in the larger scheme of things. In time, the girl gave birth to two children, Sikandar and Shakuntala. Her children called her Amma, and this name stuck.

In the Mountains

"So you are Amma's daughter, and a direct descendant of the courtesans of Karim Street!" Megan's green eyes sparkled with excitement. "Bua, that's so *cool.* But why did you stop? Tell me about my mother, tell me how you guys met and became friends."

Shakuntala turned away from Megan to look at the remains of the fire, the dead embers scattered in the courtyard, the dark, lifeless pile of soot.

"Your mother tourist, my brother tour guide," she said, pulling herself up from the *charpai* with a groan. "See city, come my home, we friends. Now I sleep."

"Come on, you can't do this," Megan said, disappointed. "Such a long story about the courtesans, and just *two lines* for my mother?"

"I not know…more. I sleep," Shakuntala repeated stubbornly, draping her shawl over her head and shuffling into the house. Behind her stretched an irresolute silence, questions hanging mid-air like the winged creatures of night.

Megan stared at the older woman's retreating back. "That's so not fair," she muttered.

"I understand your frustration. So sorry," Naina said, walking up to Megan. "Bua can be very moody. I will try to speak to her…"

"Don't *you* know anything?" Megan asked, her eyes hopeful. "About my mother, I mean. About her time in India."

Naina shook her head. "I wish I did," she said, wringing her hands in distress. "But no. Nothing important. I can't help you, really."

"Hey, that's okay," Megan smiled wanly. "You tried your best. Don't be upset, please. I can come again later. At least we broke the ice. Besides, I really enjoyed Bua's story. Even if it was so over the top. I mean, it can't have been so marvellous and magical, so completely gender-equal!"

"Is there complete gender-equality even today?" Naina asked softly. "Do you have that in America?"

Megan was quiet. "Probably not," she replied eventually. "That was a knee-jerk reaction, I guess. Because I tend to think of women's choices and women's freedom as only possible in a modern context."

"I understand. And believe me, I don't buy Bua's entirely glossy version of the courtesans either. The daily drudgery of marriage, yes, but perhaps some of those women wanted it. Convention, respectability, all that. Even failed love sounds less painful in Bua's version than it actually is...." Naina's voice trailed off.

"I think there would have been some abuse and exploitation too," Megan cut in. "The patrons were powerful guys—I can't imagine them being endlessly obliging! But what really saddened me was the thought of how the situation must have worsened after colonisation."

"Bua did mention that, right?"

"Yeah, but we more or less glided over the horrible racism of that time. What did it mean for the courtesans to have to make themselves available to the coloniser? To lay their bodies open to sex, to medical inspection, to laws?"

"True," Naina conceded.

"And all this to keep the military virile and marching towards the expansion of Empire! What happened to the women afterwards, that's what I want to know! In fact, I don't think it was very different from slavery in America—black women eroticised, abused, discarded. No, the real story must have been far, far worse. Before the British, after the British."

"Agreed. But the good parts are not all fantasy either."

"No, no, I agree with you there. Believe it or not, Bua's story is making me think about a lot of stuff. About history, modernity, the east and the west. This is the problem of being an academic—one thinks too much!"

Naina smiled, pulling her shawl closer as a swirl of mist rolled into the courtyard.

"It's getting cold. I should really go," Megan said, looking at her watch.

"Er...maybe you should take back the...the shawls and other things you got for us," Naina said, biting her lip. "You didn't get what you came for, so it's not right for us to accept gifts from you."

Megan looked at her, startled. These are good people, she thought guiltily. It's my fault for digging up long-buried worlds, digging up the ground beneath everyone's feet. "Naina, there is no question of it," she said softly. "A gift once given cannot be taken back. Surely you know that?"

Naina nodded, feeling more miserable than ever. How, oh how, was she going to do what Bua wanted her to, and ask Megan to return that other gift from so long ago?

"What's the matter with you? What are you looking so worried about?"

"Nothing," Naina lied. "Just wondering how you will get back to your hotel. It's quite late."

"Oh, don't worry, I had asked the hotel to send a cab for me. It's waiting round the corner."

"You know, I wanted to ask…I mean…" Naina muttered, feeling dizzy all of a sudden."

"Yes?" Megan prompted. She suddenly felt weary, travelling so far for a story she couldn't find, travelling in sadness, through the middle mists of time. "What is it?"

Naina took a deep breath. Looking at Megan, she saw a beautiful, spirited woman, motherless like her. Tired from a pointless journey, shadows under her eyes. "Nothing," she said, making a quick decision. "I just wanted to say that in case I don't see you again, please enjoy the rest of your stay in Delhi."

Megan stared at her. "Are you sure there is nothing else?" she asked slowly.

Naina blinked. "What do you mean?"

"Oh, no, nothing." Megan replied quickly. "Listen, are you working tomorrow?" she asked, as a thought entered her mind. "I guess not, because it's a Sunday. Can you take Monday off?"

"Monday off?" Naina asked, surprised. "Why?"

"I'm going off to the Himalayas tomorrow. I wanted to do some ice-skating in the rinks, but I met this man at Delhi Haat who said Shimla and Mussoorie would be too crowded. He recommended this little town called Kasauli instead. No ice-skating, but a gorgeous view of the mountains. I'll be back Tuesday morning. Why don't you come with me?"

"Come with you? Oh, you mean, like…but I don't know anything about your mother," Naina said, distressed all over again.

"Heck, it's not about my mother! I won't even bring her up, I promise. It's just about a holiday with a friend," Megan explained hurriedly.

"Oh."

"I've already hired a car, and made the hotel reservations for two nights. They didn't have single rooms so I booked a double. It won't cost me a cent extra if you come."

"No, no," Naina replied, overwhelmed. "I couldn't! How could I impose on you like that?"

"And when was the last time you went for a holiday outside the city?"

Naina looked stricken. "When Babuji was alive," she almost whispered.

"Exactly," Megan said, pursing her lips and looking very resolute. "You need a holiday."

Naina was still shaking her head. "Bua won't allow me to go with...with a stranger..."

"Come on, you're not five years old! And I'm hardly a stranger. Bua and my mother were friends, remember—even if she won't talk about her now. Besides, I don't have any close girlfriends, not since high school, so I have *years* of girl-talk waiting inside me! Please come, Naina. It'll be fun for me, and a change of scene for you."

Naina breathed deeply. "Okay," she said quietly. "But I have to ask Bua's permission first."

As if on cue, there came a resounding shout from within the walls of the haveli. "You go, go, Bua no stop. *Hepy* holiday."

✦

Their hotel perched whitely on a hillock, its large, soaring balconies like the wings of an exotic bird. All around rose the hills, icy and obdurate, here and there a wind-strangled tree, caves and secret hollows, an unending sense of sky.

Naina leaned against the balcony and breathed in the sweet scent of pines. "It's beautiful here, isn't it?" She turned to Megan, who was fiddling with the coffeemaker. "So clean, and so much silence. No metallic sounds from factories, no garbage, no bus fumes."

"My dad's house is like this," Megan said with a smile. "It's in a place called Pennington, on the outskirts of Princeton. Very quiet, just flowers and birds and deer."

After their initial early morning enthusiasm, the two women had each lapsed into their own world of dreams and desperations, and the seven hour drive from Delhi to Kasauli had gone by in near-silence.

It was only after their car inched into the upper altitudes that they had burst forth in excitement, and now, ensconced in a plush heritage hotel and totally rejuvenated from an errant afternoon siesta, there was suddenly so much to talk about.

"You probably don't have places like this in America. I mean, like hill stations?"

"No, we don't have the concept of 'hill stations' like you guys," Megan replied. "These cantonments were created in the colonial era, you were saying?"

"Yes, so the European officers could escape the summer heat with their families."

"We go to the hills mostly for skiing and stuff. Like the Pocanos, or Vermont. I went to the Pocanos four times with my ex-boyfriend. I don't ski, so I was totally bored."

"Then why did you keep going back?"

Megan laughed. "That's a good question, I guess. Well, so my ex – his name was William, and he refused to shorten it – didn't concern himself too much with other people's feelings. He liked to ski, so we went for him. We mostly did what he wanted to do."

"Sounds like someone I used to know," Naina said wryly. "What happened then? With your ex-boyfriend?"

"Nothing," Megan replied tersely. "After two years of my making an absolute fool of myself, he decided he wanted to remain with his wife after all."

"He was married?" Naina asked, horrified.

"I know. It does sound awful," Megan said, looking away. "But, well. He was a brilliant, distinguished scholar, much celebrated in academic circles. We had almost two decades of age difference between us. When he began pursuing me vigorously, I couldn't believe my luck. So yours truly, who'd never had too much time for men, fell head over heels!"

"Hmm. Where did you meet?"

"At a conference in New York. I the gullible graduate student from Princeton, he the charismatic keynote speaker from the host university. I thought he was the most passionate, sensitive, cultured man I had ever met!"

"I know that feeling," Naina said, remembering how giddy she'd felt when Varun had held open a door for her the first time. They still swamped her sometimes, the smells of that evening. Of fresh manure sprinkled in the garden, the sickly-sweet scent of *juhi* flowers clinging to the vines that trembled along the sides of the bungalow, the stench of burnt cake from the kitchen.

"And it lasted for two whole years! Hell, I even wanted him to be the external member on my Ph.D committee. Thank God my father stepped in at that point. He's a pretty cool dad, not one to interfere in our lives except in a fun way, but that one time, he sat me down and made me diss my crazy plan."

"Why? What would have happened otherwise?"

"Oh, who knows? There are so many stories of grad students just going *under* because of unsupportive committees. Maybe he would have failed me because I had stopped giving him blowjobs or something," Megan muttered dubiously, chuckling to see Naina redden. "Aw, come on! Don't tell me you've never done anything with a guy!"

"Yes, I have," Naina replied quietly, thinking of how Varun would pull her into corridors, closets, kitchens, her awkward fumbling, his expensive cologne and practised charm. Their urgent couplings, the steely rasp of zips, buttons flying everywhere, and afterwards, such emptiness.

Outside, the light was fading and the mountains looked like grave old men, wrinkled faces and crooked elbows, their heads bent together. Curls of smoke were rising up from the settlements at the foot of the hills, and the aching languor of the hills made Naina shiver. "His name was Varun. He is married now. To the daughter of one of his father's friends. I hope he holds her close after they...make love. I hope he gives her tenderness, and truth."

"Why, did he lie to you?"

"He said he loved me, that he wanted us to be together. But it's not completely his fault. It's mine too. I wanted so much to be loved, to be married...to not have to worry about finances all the time. I believed everything he said. Even though...even though his actions spoke otherwise."

"I hear you. It was the same with me. All of William's stories about how he was totally incompatible with his wife, how she had already moved on, how his love for me was greater than he'd ever felt for *any* woman *ever*," Megan said, pacing the balcony. "Six months into our relationship, I found a lipstick mark on his shirt. Couldn't have been his wife's; she was the no-lipstick type. But I let it go, told myself I was making a mistake. Afterwards, I heard stories about his other affairs, all with his students. He liked them young. Put him with a bunch of young girls, and he was like a kid in a candy store. When I asked him, he denied everything outright. All rumours, he said."

Naina looked at Megan sympathetically. "How did the relationship end?"

"Ah. When all the empty 'Once I am a free man' talk got too much, I said I needed him to go ahead and file for that godamned divorce. He hummed and hawed for a week, two weeks. Then one day, I spotted him and his wife at Macy's."

"Macies?"

"It's this famous departmental store in New York. So well, they didn't see me. She must have been in her late forties, very dignified. She seemed quite...motherly too, you know, like kind and generous. And they didn't necessarily look unhappy either. I was so angry with him, with myself. Afterwards, I remembered his wife's eyes and felt a strange sort of affinity with her. It's hard to explain...but I was like, if he could cheat on you, of course he can cheat on me! Next day, I called it off."

Naina reached out and took Megan's hand. "You're so strong," she whispered.

"My relationship with William wouldn't exactly make the founding mothers of feminism swell with pride," Megan responded wryly. "I guess I was strong in calling it off...but the funny thing with strength is that not every day is the same. Some days I would end up thinking of him, and hating myself for it..."

"I understand. No matter who ends the relationship, it's always...hard."

"It could have been harder, I guess. But I had my dissertation defense, and later, a new job, a new city."

The two women sat in silence, sipping on their coffee while a sharp wind whittled the branches of the trees outside. "Maybe marrying him would have been worse than letting him go?" Naina offered after a while. "When I feel really sad, that's what I say to myself."

"Oh, *totally*! I totally get how I was super lucky to have been denied his lifelong companionship!" Megan chuckled. "So, moving on to happier things, did you meet anyone else after that guy?"

Naina thought of Shekhar, his earnest smile, his passion for the old city. "No," she said, shrugging the thought off. "I don't think so."

"Why? Because the courtesans of Karim Street only love once?"

"Keep quiet," Naina said, turning red. "I did meet someone, but he's...he's a friend of Varun's. Friends are like each other, aren't they? Birds of a feather?"

"Sometimes. Not always. Do they *seem* alike?"

"No, probably not. He's nice, not pretentious at all. And we have...other things in common."

"Then what's stopping you? Wait, don't tell me, I know. Inertia. And the little part inside us that is afraid to be hurt again."

Naina nodded. "And what about you?"

Megan laughed. "The same inertia. Should have started dating again, but well. Though I *will* say...."

Here she paused, wondering how to frame her relationship with Kevin in a way that would be fair to her, to him. "It's my best friend," she said finally. "I've known him since high school. My dad loves him, he's always there for me, all that. But there's a problem."

"I know. You're not attracted to him, right?"

"Well, no, it's not exactly like that," Megan said uncomfortably, a flush creeping up her neck at the warm memory of his lips on hers. "I suppose it didn't *occur* to me to think of him that way for the longest time, but then, you know how..."

Naina gave a delighted whoop. "You *like* him! Best friend! The best, best. You found your love story!"

"Shut up, will you," Megan murmured. "I'm still confused. Funny how we're never confused about the douchebags, the cheaters, the weaklings. It's the good guys that confuse us and get us thinking!"

Naina giggled. "You're right. And all this talk has made me hungry," she said, clutching her stomach and making Megan grin.

"Me too. How about ordering a nice shepherd's pie for dinner? And some wine—oh, for *God's sake*, don't get all pious and whine about how you don't drink! I'll get you some apple juice and you can pretend it's a bourbon."

Later, dinner over, the floor an intricate geometry of plates and empty bottles, Megan passed up the idea of coffee. "Okey dokey, I need to crash," she pronounced amicably to the bathroom mirror, and crash she did, sloppy grin, tousled hair, hairbrush in hand.

Naina looked at her new 'friend' – yes, that warm, molten word had seeped into her heart with such ease – and smiled. Outside, it had begun to snow again, humped white rocks everywhere, the shadows of shivering trees twisted like ribs. Turning away from the window, the lonely whistle of a nightbird somewhere behind her, Naina threw some more logs of wood into the fire. Then she settled back into the armchair by the fireplace to watch the bright orange flames dance.

✦

"Wake up, Naina. I've ordered chicken sandwiches and Spanish omelettes, and I'm making another pot of coffee. Wake up!"

Naina sat up in bed with a start. "What? Oh, what time is it?" she asked, still groggy. "When did I get in bed?"

"You didn't. You went off to sleep in the armchair. I got up for some water at night, and pretty much dragged you to bed. It's two!"

"Two…? Two in the *afternoon*?"

"Yes, sweetheart. You must have slept for at least fourteen hours. Do you feel rested?"

"Rested, rested, yes!" Naina yelled like a schoolboy, standing up on the bed, picking up her pillow and throwing it at Megan.

"What the hell! Did all that sleep drive you *insane* or something?" Megan said, delighted to see this freer side of Naina. Putting her coffee mug down, she climbed onto the bed. "Too bad, because in Bed State, we kill off our mad. Oh, you're so, so dead!"

Afterwards, lying underneath a massacred mound of bedclothes, their laughing faces turned up towards the sloping wooden beams of the ceiling, Naina suddenly turned serious. "We'll stay friends, won't we? Even after you go back?"

"Of course," Megan replied, surprised. "Of course we'll remain friends. Now tell me, how do you want to spend the afternoon? I've been poring over a map. We can either walk to the right, to Monkey Point, or to the left, towards the bazar. There's a club here too. Tennis courts, snooker, a good bar, that sort of thing. It would be nice to have a cosmopolitan. Dunno if they'll let us in without a membership though."

"You are an alcoholic," Naina calmly pronounced, getting up from bed. "Oh, it's so *cold*!"

"Lemme turn up the heat some more. And you, go put on that heavy woollen thing you got, the bristly brown one that looks like a dead horse."

Naina giggled. "Let's go to the bazar," she said. "I want steaming hot ginger tea. And kachoris, if they have them."

The bazar – or mall, as it was called – was a colourful line of shops sloping all the way down the road and into the main part of town. Clothes, beautiful handbags, shoes, umbrellas, even electronics. But what really caught the two women's attention were the handicrafts whittled out of wood. Naina bought two small candleholders for her aunt and a large one for Megan with 'Dear Friend' etched on it, while Megan bought a wooden wall-hanging with painted flowering vines swirling into the words 'Remember Me.'

Afterwards, they guzzled crispy hot kachoris and potato sabzi, washing it all down with tall glasses of buttermilk. This part of town was narrow, more crowded, adults in monkey caps, children buttoned up like snowmen. Every few minutes, sprays of snow from the previous night slid off the naked branches overhead, onto the road, and someone slipped on the slush with a groan. A man in dyed hair and a purple windbreaker had been eyeing the two women for quite some time as they sat on a roadside bench slurping their buttermilk; when he swaggered past them, skeetered dangerously on the snow, and went rolling down the hilly road, Naina threw back her head and laughed.

"I've not seen you laugh like this before," Megan said with a smile. "When I first met you, you had such an air of sadness."

"I haven't felt so happy in a long time. Maybe I just needed to get away from the city. Thank you. For bringing me with you."

"Tell me something—and only because we've been talking so frankly. Did you stop dancing because your relationship ended? You don't have to answer if you don't want to."

"It's okay. I can tell you. It was partly because of that—"

"I thought as much," Megan cut in, her eyes hardening. "I stopped dancing too, do you know? After William."

"You *dance*? What dance?"

"Nothing as fancy as you. I used to learn ballet as a kid, but I quit years ago. Still, I used to like to go dancing on the weekends. Just normal stuff."

"In my case, it wasn't only because of him though," Naina said, reflecting. "Once upon a time, I wanted to be a professional dancer and choreographer. Gave some public performances too..."

"So what happened?"

"Too much politics. Opportunities are few, you have to curry for favours. You know how they speak of the casting couch in movies? I've seen it happen in the classical dance industry too..."

"No kidding!"

Naina nodded. "Maybe it's in every industry. Who knows? Ultimately, it's the well-connected ones who get ahead. Empanelment, foreign tours, politics everywhere. I got so fed up. Bua feels sad, but she doesn't realise my own sadness. I loved dance."

"I understand," Megan said quietly. "But what now? You couldn't possibly *never* dance again. Or is that..."

"No, no. I want to do...something."

"One of my brothers' friends won a fellowship. In the creative arts. She's super excited. Going off to Paris."

"Nice."

"Listen, why don't *you* apply for something like that?" Megan asked, her eyes brightening. "Where you can collaborate with international artists, choreograph pieces, put across a unique point of view?"

"I had thought of that once," Naina said slowly. "After a performance I saw, a fusion of Kathak and Ballet. Breathtaking, it was. I got goose bumps. I'm serious."

"Exactly! Creative improvisation. Art needs to transcend boundaries, craft new forms, new audiences."

"But where would I start? Oh, I know. It's what my students do. Google…" Naina laughed.

"Yup, run a combination of searches—dance, fellowship, that sort of thing. You have internet at home?"

"Internet at home! I don't even have a computer. But I did learn how to use one. And there is a cyber-café opposite the music school. Let's see…"

An hour of people-watching went by, until the standing light of the afternoon lay pink and low, spreading thinly into the creased corners of the sky. The wind was icy-cold, and in the distance, the mountains loomed like friendly giants, their oversized heads swirling in the fog. "Seems like it might snow again later. Go back?" Megan asked.

When Naina nodded, they picked up their bags and began walking back in silence up the winding road. On their way they passed a young man with a flock of sheep, the oldest grave, the youngest spindly-legged and frisky. The bells around the sheep's necks rang all the way down the mountain road, its music immediate and alive.

"Those bells sound like the bells of the *ghungroo*," Naina said earnestly. "They're even in rhythm, can you hear? I could move my feet to their beat…" She did an impromptu step, on a patch cleared of snow.

"Kathak? Fascinating! What do you do with the hands?"

"This," Naina clasped her palms together, moving her arms in a stylised way, first one, then the other, the fingers nimble and graceful.

Soon her hips were arching and she was doing pirouettes, her entire body moving in rhythm.

"Beautiful," Megan said, enjoying the moment. "Give me the beat."

"*Ta thai thai tat, aa thai thai tat*," Naina began, not stopping her dance.

Nodding, Megan clicked her fingers to the beat. When she joined in with ballet-like steps, Naina gave a whoop of delight. The two women moved their hips and hands, pirouetting side by side. A woman balancing a basket of twigs on her head came down the mountain road; seeing the two women, she stared and giggled. Against a spectacular backdrop of snowy hills, Naina and Megan continued to dance.

It was a full five minutes later, when an army jeep passed, followed closely by a tourist van, that they stilled their movements. One of the men seated inside the van hooted. "*Naacho, mat ruko*," he yelled as the brightly-painted van turned a corner and disappeared from view.

"What did he say?" Megan asked, hand on her hip, breathing hard.

"Dance, don't stop," Naina translated, red-faced.

Starting to laugh, the two women collapsed on the side of the hill. Soon Megan was laughing much harder.

"What's the matter?" Naina asked.

"It struck me that you are so much a courtesan of Karim Street," Megan teased. "Green eyes, love of dancing, fixation with one man, the works!"

"That way, even you are a Karim Street courtesan!" Naina replied crossly. "Green eyes, love of dancing. Even fixation with one man, remember?"

"That's true. Now why didn't I think of that?" Megan asked, mock-serious. Afterwards, she would marvel that Naina's words hadn't reminded her of the letter and darkened her mood. But that afternoon was magical, with no space for self-doubt or sorrow.

And so the two women looked at each other and started giggling again, their laughter flying over the gabled roofs of the church, the tops of firs and pines, higher, up the sides of the mountains and into the shimmering brightness beyond.

An Ending and a Beginning

"Enjoy your evening," Megan yelled, waving wildly from the car.

It had snowed heavily in Kasauli the past night. Morning, the snow sat still and obstinate on the edges of the town, blocking the main road in places and delaying their departure by almost six hours. It was late evening by the time they reached Delhi, the streetlamps flinging circles of light onto rain-slickened roads.

Naina waved back, waiting until the car was out of sight before turning to walk into the Vaderas' house. "Hello Aunty," she said to Neelima, who was standing purposefully in the driveway as usual.

"Hi *beta*. You're late, very late."

"Sorry, Aunty. Had gone for a holiday...we got late getting back."

"Holiday?" Neelima pounced on the word, her eyes narrowing. "Where? With whom?"

Naina exhaled. "Kasauli. With a friend from America."

"Yes, yes, I saw a *firang* in that car with you. Why didn't you ask her in?"

Oh. Because I like her and I don't like you. "She was in a hurry. Er...important meeting."

"Oh, okay, okay."

Naina smiled to think of the pious reaction of members of the Vadera family to words such as 'meetings,' a heavyweight word in these circles, a word that probably stood for handshakes, hefty sums of money, heights of power, hidden enemies. Naina's parents, on the other hand, would have merely smiled, and her Bua would simply spit some more betel juice on the nearest wall. "I'll go up to Vartika now, Aunty," she said, beginning to walk away.

"Yes, yes. And Naina..." Neelima called out, very loudly, to Naina's back "...Varun and Karishma will be here today. For the weekend. The boy misses his mother, can you imagine..."

For once, Naina didn't bother to look back.

For the next hour and a half, she found her mind darting off to Kasauli again and again, to the mountain's silvery, white-topped summits, the church with its diamond face, the bazar, the laughing days, the pine-scented silence of the nights.

"You look happy today," Vartika remarked, once their *riyaaz* was over. "All smiley smiley."

"Why, don't I smile on other days?"

"You do. But you have sad eyes."

Naina cocked her head to one side. "I *feel* happy today," she said, giving the younger girl a hug.

Afterwards, coming down the stairs, she thought she could hear Karishma's high, distinct voice. Oh, they are here already. Just my luck, Naina thought, consternation spiralling into concern when she stepped into the foyer and heard muffled sobs. She was wondering whether to go into the living room and see what the matter was, or to stick to her employee status and mind her own business, when Neelima emerged.

"Oh, you're done with the *riyaaz*, good, good," she said, her face unnaturally bright.

"Is everything okay, Aunty?" Naina ventured tentatively.

"...What? Yes, yes, fine," Neelima replied, her eyes blank. "Varun and Karishma...a tiff, yes, small tiff, nothing unusual for married couples. You must be getting late. Your part of Delhi is not at all safe for girls."

"No part of Delhi is safe for girls," Naina responded dryly. "I just..."

Karishma strode out of the living room, elbowing past them to run upstairs. She looked puffy-eyed and pasty, and had put on weight, her armpits bulging out of a sleeveless blouse.

"I'll be going now," Naina said to Neelima, who was staring at Karishma distractedly.

She'd walked through the foyer and down the driveway when a familiar car stopped outside the gate and Varun stepped out. Naina averted her eyes, hoping to walk past him.

But he had spotted her. "Naina," he called, staggering towards her.

He's drunk, Naina realised in dismay. "Hi," she said, continuing towards the main gate without breaking her stride.

"So now you don't even want to talk to me?" he asked, blocking her path. "Me, the Bad Guy..." His words were slurred, his eyes red and unfocused. The top button of his shirt hung loose, like his lower lip.

She pulled her shawl closer around herself. "Varun. Just let me go. You know there's no point in..."

"Yeah, that's right. No point. No point at all," he said. "Is Karishma inside? Are you going home? Can I drop you?"

"You're in no condition to drive, and I wouldn't have let you even if you were. And yes, your *wife* is inside," Naina replied pointedly. "She didn't look too happy."

"That's me. I do that to everyone. Didn't you know?"

Naina took a long breath. "Varun, I think you should..."

"Ha. Should. Best word in the world, isn't it? Varun, you should ace this deal, you should double the company's profits in that quarter… you, you should know the most important people in the city, be the best bloody husband to your whining wife. Should, should, fucking should!"

Naina forced herself to look at him. She had waited for this chance for so long, the chance to face him squarely. And when she finally had it, here he was, unkempt and inebriated, robbing her of the one last thing she'd still held on to—her anger. For a desperate moment, she tried to remember the love again, the laughter, the passion and the promises. But instead of the past, she found herself thinking of how cold the evening had turned, and how dark, a mist touching her temples with moist fingers. She tried again, and all she could remember was that a car waited outside the gate, and that the car could take her home.

"You remember how you used to run your fingers through my hair?" Varun was saying. "Do that for me again, please…"

Her eyes dimmed. "Shhh," she said, touching her palm to his forehead. It was burning. "You have fever, Varun. You should go in and lie down."

His shoulders slumped. Gently, she ran her fingers through his hair, sweeping it back with soft strokes like she used to. He whimpered like a child, closing his eyes. Outside the gates, the car's headlights had turned on.

"Okay, then. I listened to you, now you listen to me. Go inside, go to bed. Morning will be better," she said.

Nodding, he opened his eyes, looked at her for a long time, and stumbled off.

She kept staring at his retreating back even after he had disappeared from view. Then, exhaling deeply, she began to walk towards the gate. "Shekhar," she called. "Wait for me."

At the steering wheel, Shekhar looked troubled. "Didn't realise you'd seen me. Isn't it too dark?" He asked, leaning across to open the door for her.

"I recognised the car," she replied, sliding in and shutting the door. "From the other day. Will you drive me home?"

He looked unsure. "Is everything okay?"

Naina nodded, looking out of the window. She was breathing heavily and her head throbbed.

"I came to drop Varun," Shekhar continued unnecessarily. "He'd come to visit Dad, and ended up having too much to drink. I didn't mean to look at the two of you or anything… just wanted to see him get inside safely. Then…then I saw you coming out, and…"

"Will you drive me home?" Naina repeated tiredly.

"Yes. Yes, of course," Shekhar said, starting the car. Then he reached out and put his hand on her shoulder. "Listen, if you still have feelings for him, maybe you both can…I mean, I don't think his marriage is working out, and maybe this time he will…"

To Naina, Shekhar's words sounded like a gong. It's strange how, for all of life's endless agitations and the long litanies that are put off until tomorrow, the final moment of reckoning ultimately only takes a split-second. This is my split-second, Naina decided. "Can you wait for me, please? I'll be back," she said urgently, unlocking her door again, stepping out and starting to run back into the house.

"What…"

"Just wait, please," Naina threw back, breathless.

In the living room, Neelima Vadera sat creating a flower arrangement of vivid blue orchids, roses and ferns. She looked up as Naina entered. "Naina…? Did you forget something?"

Yes, my brain. Can I please have it back? "Aunty, I wanted to talk to you."

"Oh. What about?"

About that garish flower arrangement. Please don't use the red roses; try some white flowers instead. "My job. I am sorry I...er...cannot continue."

"...What?" Neelima asked, putting her pair of scissors down on the table and waving a bunch of ferns at Naina. "*Why*? What happened?"

"Personal reasons, Aunty."

"Tell me, tell me. Maybe I can help?"

Naina smiled softly. "Thank you, but no, I have to help myself. It's towards the end of the month, so I was thinking if you could just pay me my salary..."

Neelima stared at Naina. "Why don't you go home and think about the job, *beta*? Maybe you will change your mind tomorrow?"

That's what I am afraid of. "No Aunty, I won't change my mind."

"What is this, Naina?" the older woman coaxed. "Vartika needs you, you know that."

At the mention of the girl, Naina bit her lip. "I know. I am really sorry," she said, her face small. "Vartika has my phone number. If she...if she needs my help for a few weeks before you can find another teacher, please send her to my house. I won't charge you any fees."

Neelima gasped. "As if there are no other music teachers in the city! And no fees, what is that? Are we bankrupt or something? Really, Naina, I am *most* disappointed in you, *most* disappointed."

"I'm sorry," Naina repeated stiffly.

"Wait here. I will get you your money," Neelima spat. Going inside her room, she came out with her purse. "Here," she said, counting out hundred-rupee notes and thrusting them into Naina's hand without bothering about an envelope.

"Thank you, Aunty. Good night," Naina said, turning away. In the foyer, she stopped and glanced upstairs. No, a conversation with Vartika at this point would be very upsetting for both of them. She would miss her student: her talent, her tenacity, her tenderness. But Vartika was growing older, Naina mused; in time, she would learn to distil the good from the bad and to make her own decisions. At that point, it might even be possible for the two of them to resume their relationship outside of the calculus of power and privilege. Naina glanced around the house one last time. Then, head held high, she walked out.

In the car, Shekhar looked crestfallen. When Naina emerged, he opened the door for her again. "How did it go? Is he feeling better?" he asked, trying his best to smile.

"Who?" Naina asked, surprised. "Varun, you mean? Oh, I hadn't gone inside to speak to *him*!"

Shekhar looked confused. "I thought…"

"No. I went to speak with Aunty. I have left the job."

"…You *have*? Really?"

"Yes. You do understand?"

Shekhar was quiet. "Yes, I do," he said eventually. "I think you did the right thing. It must have taken a lot of courage." Then, with a shy smile, he drummed the dashboard of the car. "Shall we go now?"

Weeks later, she would giggle at how the scene had played out like a predictable Bollywood film: Exit Hero One, Enter Hero Two. There hadn't even been an interval in-between; instead, the new one had waited in the car while she'd said goodbye to the old one. But in that moment, all she could think was that no matter how wretched one's life, God gives everyone at least one magical evening, an evening when the stars shine brighter and things go right and the heart can shed its load and look forward to a new dawn.

As the headlights of passing cars lighted up Shekhar's face, his strong chin and his kind eyes, she found herself smiling back at him. "Yes."

✦

Megan had just finished ordering a cheesesteak from room service, and now sat propped up in bed flicking TV channels. Ah, here was something familiar, she thought with a grin, when she saw chef Bobby Flay and his gutsy Japanese challenger on *Iron Chef America,* furiously plating the five-course meals they had prepared over the last hour. Spinach was the mystery ingredient this time. With the giant clock in Kitchen Stadium ticking like a bomb, the two chefs lined up their spinach tamales, spinach and oyster bisque, spinach-wrapped kobe beef, spinach and feta soufflé, spinach yuzu saké, and even spinach ice-cream. Ten minutes later, a panel of hungry judges declared the challenger higher on plating and originality, but Flay higher on taste. As the credits began to roll, and a bright voice announced "Coming up next—Rachel Ray cooks with the celebrity international chef for this week," Megan got up to get a can of juice from the fridge.

In the background, she could hear Ray giving her studio audience a sunny, spirited welcome. "And now we have our guest chef for the week, all the way from the land of cumin and curry—India. He owns three successful restaurants in New Delhi, Mumbai and Tokyo, has authored over a dozen bestselling cookbooks, and has lectured at culinary institutes worldwide. Guys, a big round of applause for Chef Balbir Singh." Megan took a sip of the juice, turned around and stared. It was her bearded friend from Delhi Haat, the one who had pulled her leg and lectured her relentlessly on Indian cuisine!

Megan looked more closely. Yes, it was definitely him. As Chef Singh's eyes twinkled and he began to speak about his greatest passion, food, she couldn't help laughing. She had had lunch with one of India's most celebrated chefs! God, this was unbelievable. And now he was on a show in her country, with one of America's most celebrated chefs.

On the show, Chef Singh was speaking of fusion cuisine and spices going global. "So for starters, I have for you a tweaked version of a popular Indian street food – the *gol gappa* – which we will serve with brandy instead of the traditional spicy water. The main course is my Indian take on the classic American surf and turf, with marinated shrimp on a bed of *kabab*s and a wasabi raita sauce, and for dessert there is flambéd gulab jamun. So let's begin!"

As the audience cheered, Megan was reminded of her earlier conversation with Kevin, about how diasporas were a thing of the past, and how the globe was shrinking so close everyone had to learn to be a traveller, at home anywhere in the world. Oh damn, she missed Kevin—

A discreet knock on the door interrupted her thoughts. "Come in," Megan called out, smiling at the waiter wheeling in a small trolley with the cheesesteak, a bottle of sparkling water, and a vase with a single rose. "Smells great," she said appreciatively. Moments later, she was tucking in heartily into the cheesesteak. Kevin liked his with extra bell peppers, she remembered.

The trip to the hills with Naina had made her think a lot about him. *Maybe that's what I really needed*, she thought, *some girl-talk to get it all straight….*

After the plates were cleared, she dialled his cell number. Kevin's voice came on almost immediately, very brisk and business-like. "Hullo?"

"Hey," she said, feeling elated to hear his voice. In that moment, all she wanted was to hug him, put her head on his shoulders, watch the sunset, whatever. It didn't matter what they did; just being with him made her happy, always had. If there had been even a shadow of doubt in her mind, all vestige of it was wiped away. In that precise moment, she *knew*. "Wassup?"

"...Meg? Is that you?" he said, sounding surprised. "Where are you calling from?"

"New Delhi. Where are you?"

"Beijing, I'm in Beijing. Listen, it's great you called. I was thinking about you, your trip. What's goin' on?"

"Making friends, exploring new places, having a blast. And you?"

"Work, mostly. Haven't had too much time to explore China, but I plan to over the weekend. Hell, I still can't believe we are both so far away from home. And around the same time too!"

"I know. So did you miss me?"

There was silence on the other end. "Sure,..." he said guardedly.

"How much?"

"What's this? Some dumb game?"

"No. I'm dead serious. How much?"

"Listen, Meg, I've had a long day, so maybe..."

Megan took a deep breath. "Kevin, will you go out with me?" she asked, closing her eyes while her heart thudded madly in her chest.

"...What?"

"I'm asking you out, you idiot."

A minute of silence, exquisite and unbearable. Then, suddenly, Kevin was laughing. "You really are serious, aren't you? God, I'd even stopped hoping! Everyone says once you're in the friend zone, there's absolutely no chance. What *happened*?"

"I just got it, that's what happened. No friend zone anymore. I have butterflies," she grinned. "I swear. We can cue the violins and fireworks about now."

"I want to come to India right now just to kiss you. Shit, I can't. Too much work here, and these project deadlines—"

"Don't worry about it. I'll be back home before New Year's. I'll see you then."

Kevin was still laughing. "Ever the feminist, aren't you? You had to be the one to ask *me* out!"

"Have a problem?"

"Nope." Kevin replied with a chuckle. "But hey, I still can't believe it. We're going to be so happy, you know that?"

"Well, I don't know," she said, eyes twinkling. "I think we'll have some godawful rows..."

An hour later, Megan was kissing him goodnight with the promise of calling back the next evening. Soon afterwards, lying in the bathtub, she couldn't stop smiling. What an awesome week, she thought. I've seen a beautiful country, made a great friend, and my love life is pretty sorted too. There's still the stuff I don't know, but maybe that's how it should be. Maybe it's not important, and never was.

Okay, I am about ready to return home now.

Her skin glistening, a fragrant sea of bubbles dancing around her, she smiled to think of how she and Naina had danced on a slippery mountain road the previous day. Dad says I get my love of dancing from you, Mother, she suddenly thought. Like Naina gets hers from the courtesans. I didn't know you well at all, but I hope you danced enough in your life, Mother. I hope you danced enough.

Excerpts from a Diary

Sikandar teases me relentlessly and calls me his courtesan. It's the colour of my eyes and my love for dancing, he says. On cue, I do a Kathak step, a little pirouette I had learnt from Amma, and then lift my flowing skirt to show him my new anklets from Dariba Kalan. His eyes become serious and clouded; you're beautiful, he says, in his deep, gravelly voice.

We had planned to walk around the old city until evening. But the monsoon has arrived early this year and the heavens had to burst, turning afternoon into night. Running in the rain, we seek shelter in his house. I had hoped to get a change of clothes from Shakuntala, but she is sleeping and so is Amma; the house is very quiet and we speak in whispers as we tiptoe up the stairs to his room.

Sikandar gives me a towel, and I stand drying my hair by the window. The sky is a wet, quivering purple, and I can see lightning streaking across roofs and treetops, its ends bright and arrow-like. Why doesn't Shakuntala like me, I ask.

Sikandar smiles; surely you understand, he says. Can you imagine Shakuntala's woe, having spent all her life ruing that she neither has green eyes nor any dancing talent, and suddenly being faced with a green-eyed woman who loves to dance?

Well, my apologies to your sister, I respond huffily, but green eyes aren't all that rare in my country, and many people in the world like to dance.

The smell of damp earth rising from outside the window is restful, renewing. I take a deep breath and close my eyes. Then, all at once, his lips are on my eyelids, kissing their unhappy creases, their hungry, throbbing swell. And his hands are raking my hair, smoothing out the tangles, and I can tell from his sighs that he has dreamed of this for a long, long time. I want to take away your pain, all the emptiness inside you, he whispers.

I have always known Sikandar cares about me from the way he listens intently to me and lets me share my dreams with him, late into the evening, under starry skies. And even though I have never told him that my husband last touched his wife months ago, Sikandar has been able to read my story in my eyes as we have walked in the Lodhi Gardens endless times, our hands touching.

So my surprise at the suddenness of this afternoon's intimacy is giving way to an acceptance of its dark, delightful inevitability. There is no pain right now, only beauty, and peace, and grace, I murmur in response, snuggling into his arms.

My eyes are still closed when Sikandar undresses me, unbuttoning my blouse and peeling away my skirt. "*Har rag-e-khoon mein phir charaghaan ho, saamne phir woh benaqaab aaye*," he says softly. I stand in a daze while he puts his arm around my waist and gently lowers me onto his *charpai*. I feel his lips trailing kisses down the curve of my neck, the hollow of my shoulders, the rise of my breasts, the dip of my navel, and lower, lower, until I gasp. I want to give you so much pleasure, he whispers, his breath tingling against my skin, and I flush and arch my body in response.

Outside, the claps of thunder. A chill breeze blows, and I shiver. I want to remember so many things about Sikandar from the past few months...I want to remember his endless patience as he answers my naïve questions about India's history, his excitement when he shows me all the unsung nooks of Delhi, the shadows across his face as he speaks of the fate in store for his beloved old city, his passion for architecture, his kindness towards street children. But he draws me close, and all I can think of are hands and mouths and touch and taste, this spiral of pleasure, me being sucked into its vortex and screaming with joy.

Afterwards, the skies are sated, the frenzy of rain and thunder is spent, and a lazy lull descends. The afternoon is so hushed I can hear his heartbeat. He cradles me like a child and I smile. I love you, Debbie, he says then. Mmmm, I love you too, I say with feeling, I say his name.

Then I open my eyes, just in time to see the look on his face. The look whose weight I have borne for so many years, and that I will carry with me to my grave.

Mriganayani

December's end was worse than its beginning, a thick churlish fog even in the daytime, the plants in the courtyard silent and white-lipped. Shakuntala climbed up the stairs painfully. Her joints were rusty; like the hinges of the old haveli, they too would give way anytime. These stairs, when was the last time they had creaked under her feet? It must have been three years, four, Shakuntala figured, holding on to the rickety bannisters for support with one hand while clutching a small bucket of soapy water with the other. Naina used to come up once a month, to sweep the open spaces, but even she had stopped now. It hurt her to see her parents' house crumbling, the rooms with mounds of plaster fallen on the floor, the walls stripped of their gloss, skeletal.

Shakuntala reached the top of the stairs, her breathing heavy. It had been almost two weeks since Megan had visited them, two weeks since the girls had forged a friendship. Today, Megan was leaving for America, and Naina had gone to the hotel to help her pack. Afterwards, she and the new boy – what was his name, Shekhar, yes, Shekhar, a good boy, not like the other one – would go to see Megan off at the airport. Shakuntala had hoped Megan would come to see her, but why would she? These *goris,* they were all the same, just take take take...

Muttering to herself, Shakuntala walked slowly down the dusty corridor and to the furthest room on the right. There was a time when that room had been so airy, Sikandar's *charpai* in the centre, the floor tiles gleaming, books, maps of Delhi on the walls, their parents' antique bed, and brass urns filled with roses. Sikandar loved roses, red roses with their petals still smelling of morning dew. He had always tended to the rose bushes himself, even as a teenager, a green thumb that boy had, and such a heart, filled with flowers and birds and the sky. Soon after he died, his rose bushes died too, their stems shrivelled, roots rotted to the core, buds killed in the womb.

At her waist, from the string of her petticoat, hung a bunch of keys. Shakuntala pulled it out and bounced it in her palm. Was it the long one, or the short one with the corrugated edges? It had a 'B' engraved on it – that much she remembered – standing for Banarsidas *chabiwale*, the key-makers of the old city whose shop had long shut down. She peered closely but couldn't tell the markings. She really needed those glasses that Naina kept talking about...

But glasses would make her look old. Now, if they had the money for those other things, so fancy – contac, she had heard them being called, and they fit over the eyes almost invisibly – it would be a different matter. Technology was too much, Shakuntala marvelled, a solution for every problem. Well, till she got her contacs, she would have to make do with these dimming eyes—like the sunset, less light but still beautiful, she liked to think. She tried first one key, then the second, then the third. They were all rusted, ungiving metal, and she scolded each of them soundly by turn. After a few twists this way and that, the fourth one opened the door.

She had known it would be bare. During Sikandar's lifetime, he had brought his *charpai* down to the courtyard.

After his death, she had sold the rest of the furniture herself, the bookshelves, the table, the armchair. She had taken down the framed maps from the walls, taken them out of their wooden frames, rolled each one meticulously and put them in a steel trunk in the attic. She had put away the books and the brass urns too, the latter long empty but still a reminder of roses. That had been years ago. But today, unlocking the room and stepping into its dusty embrace, it struck her – the bareness, the cobwebs in the corners, the dark squares on the walls where the maps had once hung, the intricately designed tiles disappeared in filth, the urn-less, rose-less emptiness, the laughter that once was. Sighs everywhere, and echoes, the papery trail of ants through the ancient wood, the still, suspended sheets of dust, and through it all, those memories, still alive, still alive.

She could see them now, twisted under the sheets, the swan arch of her neck, his torso gleaming with beads of sweat. *Deborah*, she thought angrily. *Deborah, why you send your daughter?*

✦

"Your mother's name was Deborah, wasn't it?" Naina asked softly.

"Yes," Megan replied. "Everyone called her Debbie. Dad says I look like her."

"Bua would agree," Naina said, folding Megan's shirts and placing them neatly in the suitcase.

"Would she?"

"Yes. The first time you came home, Bua said she thought she was looking at a ghost."

"Well, I guess my mother did have green eyes," Megan said slowly.

"It's more than just the eyes. I have green eyes too, the famous Karim Street eyes, but that doesn't mean I look like your mother! No, Bua said you walked like her, talked like her...your gestures, everything."

"Interesting," Megan replied, not knowing what else to say. "Listen, Naina, now that we are friends, now that I'm *going*, can I ask you something? Why do I get the feeling that Bua didn't like my mother? When Dad gave me your address, he told me Bua and my mother were friends. But I...I didn't get that feeling at all. I've been trying to tell myself that sometimes there are just no answers, and who knows, maybe it's best that way, but...shit, Bua just didn't want to *talk* about my mother!"

"I don't know. I've wondered about that too. Maybe your mother and my *father* were closer friends. He was her travel guide, remember? And your mother met Bua through him."

"Yes, that's what Dad said too. But he also said Mother would visit your place even when your father wasn't around, to hang out with Bua, that she and Bua were friends. Maybe they fell out over something?"

"Maybe."

"Or else it's what you're saying—that she was more your father's friend. Tell me something. You don't recall him mentioning her, right? Like, ever?"

"No," Naina lied, looking away.

"Well, this bit has been tremendously frustrating, I'll tell you that."

"Do you...do you regret making this trip?" Naina asked, filled with sudden sadness.

"Of course not!" Megan reached out to lace her fingers with Naina's. "I got me a friend, remember? I wish you had a computer at home; that way I could have e-mailed you. Now I'll have to write the old-fashioned way, with paper and ink and stamps! At least I can call you; I have your number. Gimme your music school's phone number too, in case I ever need to call there."

"For that, you will have to learn to pronounce my name correctly," Naina said with a smile, "Otherwise, they won't know who you want. It's Nay-na, not Naayee-na."

"Huh. Really?" Megan asked, turning the new syllables over in her mouth. "You should have corrected me long ago. All these impossible-to-pronounce Indian names!"

Naina laughed. "You're lucky. Do you know what I might have been called instead? Mriganayani. That was my father's favourite name. Until he changed his mind and decided on Naina."

"What? Mrigan...Mrigan...hell, sounds like Megan to me," Megan said lightly. Then, as the stormy fullness of her own words washed over her like waves, delving into the depths of her past and arching up in the present, Megan swayed like a ship. The waves so big, the floors pitching and rolling, everything falling all around.

"It's time for my class," Naina was saying, moving forward to give her a hug. "I'll be back in the evening with Shekhar, before your flight. Bye, bye."

Once the doors had closed, Megan sat down on the bed, that last conversation with her father playing on her mind.

"If you've decided to go to India after all, and to meet your mother's friends, there is something else I must tell you."

"What is it, Dad?"

"The lady called Shakuntala I mentioned, that family I described as your mother's friends...Well, before your mother returned to America, they gifted her some jewels. Your mother accepted the gift, thinking they were pretty but fake. Later, we realised they were real, and worth a fortune."

"No kidding!"

"Your mother did try to return the jewels, but I believe Sikandar, the lady's brother, wouldn't hear of it. He used to make his living taking tourists on guided tours around the city. That's how your mother met him, but she soon became friends with his sister. The two women used to spend a lot of time together, I believe. Anyway, I am not sure if you should bring it up with them, or whether they will mention it first. See how it goes. All I am saying is that they were not very well off, and as unbelievably generous as their gift was, I think we should return them what is rightfully theirs..."

Megan lay back on the bed, her mind a jumble.

The anonymous letter. *You are a whore, as your mother was before you, and your grandmother. Ask anyone on Karim Street.*

The year 1981. The year her parents left India. The year she was born.

The Karim street jewels, to be passed down from one generation to the next, and never to leave the family.

Maybe your mother and my father were closer friends.

Megan, Naina, Mriganayani.

So this, dear God, was the truth. She was her mother and *Sikandar*'s daughter.

✦

Her hands shaking, Naina pushed through the revolving glass doors of the hotel. The afternoon was sunless, fog clinging to the tops of buildings and trees, people appearing from it like ghosts.

Megan. Naina. Mriganayani. No, it couldn't be a coincidence. The story that her friend had come looking for, from ten thousand miles away—this was it. The story behind Megan's questions about her mother, behind Bua's studied silence. This was the story of that box of jewels, given away by her father so long ago.

Yes, Naina had lied to Megan. Naina's father *had* mentioned Megan's mother. Once. It was around two years after Naina's mother had died. Her father had developed a cold that wouldn't go away – pneumonia, the doctors would diagnose later – and he couldn't work, not as much as he had before. Money was scarce, and one day, as he sat on his *charpai* with a bunch of bills, his sister had suddenly pounced upon him like a maddened cat. Why can't you write to that whore—yes, that was the word Bua had used, *chhinaal*, and Naina had hidden her face in confusion. Write to her and ask her to return your gift to us, Bua had spat. Enough, her brother had replied. It was the only time in her life Naina had seen her father's eyes harden like steel. I do not ever want to hear Debbie spoken about like that in this house, he had said to his sister. I do not ever want Debbie spoken about at all, is that clear? And that had been that.

After Naina's father died, and in the years that followed, Bua had spoken of the gift, but never its reasons. Sikandar had always had a large heart, she would say bitterly, large enough to give away our family jewels to some wandering *firangi* tramp who happened to have been enamoured of the story of the courtesans. Our jewels, those fabled jewels of Karim Street, gifted by Rukhsana Jan to her daughter Roshanara when the latter left Lucknow for Delhi, passed down by Roshanara to Amma, her daughter, the mother of Sikandar and Shakuntala. But Sikandar, he didn't think of his mother's sentiments, or his sister's. He didn't think of his own daughter and her birthright to the family jewels, Bua had complained endlessly.

Oh Bua, but he did think of his daughter. Not of me, because I wasn't yet born. He thought of his other daughter, the one who was about to be born. He couldn't be in her life, so he gave her his last blessing. That box of jewels, an inheritance of the women of Karim Street, was a gift from Babuji to his eldest daughter, Megan!

Sitting in the bus as it wound its way through roads crammed with vehicles, vegetable carts and people made obese by layers of warm clothes, Naina wondered if she was making an error. How could Babuji have loved Megan's mother? He had loved Naina's mother, his *wife*. So much love, apparent to all who saw it. Then how, how?

But no. Her father was not a superficial man, never had been. Nothing but the deepest feelings could account for this.... If anything, his gift to Megan's mother was proof of the highest regard he must have had for her, for their relationship. How blind I was, Naina thought, shaking her head in disbelief. Such clear bits of jigsaw, and it took me so long to piece it all together.

From the window of the bus, the afternoon sky was the colour of silt. Babuji, I respect you more today than I ever did, Naina said softly, putting her palm on her heart while her eyes filled up. If you loved Megan's mother and carried her in your heart, you never let it show. My mother and I never felt that we were sharing your love with another woman and her unborn child far away. That child, Megan, who never even got to know you.

Poor Megan. To learn that the father she loved so much, whose stories she narrated endlessly, wasn't really her father. No, Megan mustn't get to know the truth, Naina decided. The jewels should continue to be for Megan the generous gift of an artistic, impoverished man, her mother's friend from many decades ago, who walked the ruins of an ancient city and wanted nothing for himself. Megan, those jewels are a gift from our father to you, and no one shall take them away;

Babuji made sure of that in his lifetime, and I will make sure of it now. I will speak to Bua.

Bua. What does *she* know? Not much, Naina decided, because Bua wasn't one to bottle up her thoughts inside her. Oh, she might have suspected a thing or two, or else she wouldn't have called Megan's mother a whore all those years ago, but it seemed very doubtful that Bua knew anything for sure. Naina shuddered to think of what would happen if Bua did get to know the truth…Bua, who had never respected Babuji, never lost an opportunity to point out his faults to the world, and now this. No, Bua must never know. In any case, what was the point in sullying the name of people long dead? This truth, Naina resolved, would stay buried in her own heart. In any case, the courtesans of Karim Street could always keep a secret.

Naina dried her eyes and settled back against her seat. The fog outside seemed to be lifting, here and there a streak of golden light. The noises of the bus were receding into the background as she looked out of the window, a cold wind in her face. January, the trees were still bare from the winter, their long, thin branches frozen into stillness. But in a couple of months, those branches would bear leaves again, and buds. And the buds would flower, their sweet smell perfuming the old city, the new city, and all the unnamed cities in-between, and even Bua would smile. In a few months, thought Naina pleasurably, it would be spring.

✦

Why Deborah, Shakuntala continued to ask, staring as the shapes around her began to shift, taking her back, back in time.

It is many springs ago, the sky so cleansing, and she is young again. At the sound of her brother Sikandar's voice, she runs out of the room and peers down through the staircase at the courtyard below.

"See who I have brought home," Sikandar is saying in English. "Deborah." He looks up to see his sister standing upstairs, broom in hand. "Shakuntala! Come down. Meet my American friend Debbie."

Their guest looks up then, from underneath an enormous hat. She is wearing a short dress and a string of pearls around her neck, and has a corsage of flowers pinned to her bosom. She has green eyes, perfect bow-shaped lips, and her hands are like lilies. "Hi," she calls out, laughing when Shakuntala drops her broom abruptly and gets lost in a huge cloud of dust.

Shakuntala sees the way Sikandar looks at Deborah, and her heart sinks.

"Now that you have your *gori* friend, we never get to see you anymore," she complains several months later.

Brother and sister are sitting cross-legged on the kitchen floor while Amma squats on her haunches, warming aloo parathas on her ancient *angeethi*. Amma has steadfastly refused to switch over to modern cooking stoves that run on gas – all fads, and whoever heard of roasting *bhutta* on a gas stove, she spat last time at the neighbour who had dared make the suggestion – driving out the enthusiastic harbinger of new technology with colourful curses. The glowing red pieces of charcoal in the *angeethi* spit fire, as Amma drops a dollop of homemade butter on the parathas and reaches out for her jar of special cauliflower pickle to go alongside. Shakuntala's stomach rumbles.

"Earlier, the two of you came home every week. She came on her own too, to spend time with me. She said I was her friend. Liar..." Shakuntala says. "Right, Amma?"

"*Gori*, trouble, trouble," Amma grunts, her double chin wobbling. She points to the plates she wants Shakuntala to fetch, and hits her daughter with her tongs when she doesn't.

"Owww," yells Shakuntala, glaring at her mother. "Sikandar, you go get the plates!"

Sikandar obliges, as always. "This old city has so many hidden *gali*s and *kucha*s," he says to his sister afterwards. "And secret bylanes linking the old city with the new. Debbie and I spend our days exploring these..."

Sikandar's eyes remind Shakuntala of a green meadow, with tall flowers, and in their midst, a girl washed with colour. The girl wears an enormous hat and has lily hands. She laughs like a witch, the echoes of her laughter haunting Shakuntala in summer nights. "She is married, Bhai," Shakuntala finally says, her eyes imploring. She has lowered her voice so Amma cannot hear. "Don't."

Sikandar looks at his sister, in his eyes the shifting shades of surprise, guilt and embarassment. "So you...know!" he says with some effort, looking away.

"Yes. I can see it in your eyes. Love. But the *gori* will go away. I don't want to see you in pain," Shakuntala responds softly, remembering the time when Sikandar had fought an entire gaggle of neighbourhood boys because they had called his sister fat. The toughest boy of the bunch had dealt him a cuff that had split his upper lip, and his otherwise handsome face still carried a tiny scar. She looks at that scar now, and her heart brims over with love.

Sikandar shakes his head resolutely. "Debbie is the one in pain. She is trapped in her marriage. Her husband is cold and insensitive, and has no time for her. Debbie is slowly dying inside."

Shakuntala's eyes burn. I hate that woman, she thinks.

A few weeks have passed. Sikandar has been busy with other tourist groups, and maybe the *gori* has found someone else to take up her fancy. Shakuntala breathes again. But no; soon enough, Deborah sends for Sikandar.

"I'm going to meet her," he says. He is wearing his best white kurta, the one Amma had embroidered with silver conch-shell motifs that Diwali, and reeks of jasmine *ittar*.

Shakuntala holds her nose.

"Debbie likes the fragrance of jasmine," Sikandar mutters defensively. He looks distracted, but won't say why. "Tell Amma not to wait for me for lunch," he says instead. "I will be back late evening, before dinner."

Outside, dark clouds brood over the horizon like long-haired nymphs. Soon a light rain begins to fall, and the morning is mud-coloured. A few hours later, thunder rumbles across rooftops and the rain is denser, like a thick sheet of glass. Amma and Shakuntala have just finished lunch, and Amma has gone to lie down.

Shakuntala stands at her window upstairs, watching as forked tongues of lightning lick the warm sky and it sizzles. After a while, her eyelids grow heavy. She shrugs off her dupatta and climbs into bed. The rain is beating a melodious thumri on the courtyard tiles below, and she falls asleep quickly. Through the pink haze of her dreams, she hears a window shutter bang, a cough, a laugh. But there is nothing in the world as pleasurable as a rainy afternoon siesta, and she sleeps on, dreaming of peacocks and rubies and wedding processions and handsome young men waiting with garlands.

When she wakes up an hour later, the rain has abated. The afternoon is warm and fragrant with the musk of damp earth. She stretches herself leisurely and reaches for her mirror. Her complexion looks rosier, she notes with some satisfaction, but she really must make a paste of *multani mitti* and rosewater for that tiny blotch creeping up the side of her face. Somewhere a shutter bangs again; startled, she drops her mirror on the bed. The rest of the house is quiet, Amma probably still asleep in her room downstairs. Sliding into her slippers and draping her dupatta round herself, Shakuntala walks out of her room and down the corridor, checking the window shutters one by one. Ah, there it is, the wooden window shutter of Sikandar's room flapping loosely in the wind.

Shakuntala walks to the window, reaching out to close it when a movement inside takes her by surprise. But her brother isn't supposed to be back until late evening. Is it a...a *burglar*? Heart hammering, she tiptoes close and peers through the wooden beams. Oh, Sikandar is back and in bed, she realises. Her breathing returns to normal. She is about to step back when she sees a pair of pale arms snake out from under the sheets and coil around his neck. *Deborah*!

Shakuntala's eyes widen. From where she stands, mesmerised, she cannot see Deborah's face, only her brother's elated one, his light green eyes dancing with joy. Then Shakuntala hears it clearly. "Stanley." Yes, that's what Deborah says, and Shakuntala watches helplessly as Sikandar's eyes cloud over with shock and pain. "When you were... making love to me, you were thinking about...about him?" he asks Deborah wretchedly.

An unwilling witness to her brother's humiliation, and all in the span of a few seconds, Shakuntala turns away. Her eyes watering, she traces the steps back to her room and clambers jerkily into bed. I hope he can send that *gori* away from his life now, she thinks, hugging her knees. I hope she never comes back to this house again, never, never, never!

Deborah doesn't come back to their house. Not for three months. By this time, Sikandar has grown a beard and his eyes are listless. The roses in his room have wilted in their brass urns, and he refuses to let his sister plant new blooms. Then, one afternoon, there is a knock on the gate. It is she, come to say goodbye before leaving back for America with her husband.

Deborah's eyes are red-rimmed, her face pallid. When Sikandar takes her up to his room and bolts the door from inside, Shakuntala wants to tear down that door, grab Deborah by her hair and drag her out of their house. But the door opens in less than ten minutes and Deborah re-emerges, a newspaper-wrapped box in her hand. Catching a glimpse of Shakuntala, she walks down the stairs and across the courtyard. "I am going," she says quietly. "Back to America."

Good riddance, Shakuntala wants to retort. But she holds her tongue. "What?" she asks instead, pointing to the box Deborah is carrying.

"I don't know," Deborah replies, her eyes holding so much sadness that, for a moment, Shakuntala's heart almost melts. "It's a gift from your brother. He asked me not to unwrap it until later."

Shakuntala nods, standing woodenly when Deborah tries to embrace her for the last time. "When go?" she asks, looking away.

"We fly tonight," Deborah says, her lip quivering. "I will miss India, and you all."

Shakuntala nods again. Irritated that Deborah is clinging to her arm, she starts walking towards the gate.

"I will always think of you as my friend, Shakuntala. Always," Deborah whispers brokenly at the gate. Then, unable to contain herself any longer, she bursts into tears. "Oh Shakuntala, I am going to have a baby!"

Shakuntala stares at her in surprise and shock as Deborah climbs into her waiting car which drives her away, far away from their lives.

Afterwards, Shakuntala stands looking at the skies, at the black, stinging sun. Then she turns around slowly, latches the gate, and climbs the stairs up to Sikandar's room. "Open the door," she says. "I want to talk to you."

But the door remains closed.

A year passes, two years, three. Sikandar refuses to marry, and Amma is fed up. "My son receives many marriage proposals but doesn't want to get married. And my daughter wants to get married but does not receive any marriage proposals," she gossips to the milkman, the postman, and the vegetable vendors.

"Why? Why?" Everyone wants to know.

"Because my son had his heart set on a *gori* and she went back to her country, taking all our family jewels with her. And my daughter is getting fat and her eyes are plain brown and she never could dance," Amma whispers conspiratorially, scurrying away in alarm when Shakuntala comes charging, broom in hand.

One day it all gets too much for Shakuntala, and she huffs and puffs up the stairs to bang on Sikandar's door. "The baby she was carrying, it was yours, wasn't it?" she accuses, eyes ablaze. "That's why you gave our jewels to her?"

Sikandar won't look at his sister. "Go away," he mutters. "I don't know what you're talking about. Leave me alone."

"Of course I'll go away. Why don't you go away too? To America, to the woman you love! Us, Amma and me, you don't care about. So why don't you go, go!"

Shakuntala is sobbing hysterically, and Sikandar doesn't know what to do. "Shhh, shhhh, Amma will hear," he says, putting his arms around his sister. "She is so old...we don't want her to worry, do we?"

"But Amma *is* worried about you, can't you see that? Can't you see our unhappiness, can't you see us at all?" Shakuntala sobs. "Was she everything, the one who didn't care about you at all, the one who left you and went away so easily?"

Sikandar is quiet. Next day, when he appears in the morning, his mother and his sister gape. Gone are his beard, his weeks-old clothes that reeked of alcohol and angst. Instead, he is shaved and freshly showered, shining like a newly-minted coin. "I have been neglecting you, Amma," he says, hugging his mother. "I am sorry, so sorry. Who was that girl you wanted me to marry?"

"*Ya Allah, Hey Bhagwan,*" Amma says in triumph, running into the courtyard, clasping her palms together in prayer and beaming at the sky.

A year later, Sikandar is married. His new bride is very pretty and fragile, and Sikandar is attentive towards her every need. She cannot believe her good luck, and adores her husband. But every time Shakuntala sees the two of them together, her heart breaks a little. For she knows that, no matter how much he cares about his wife, Sikandar will never look at her the way he looked at Deborah Adams.

After three years, they have a daughter. When she sees the newborn's green eyes, Amma quivers with joy. "What will we name her?" she asks her son.

"Naina," Sikandar says quietly.

Shakuntala looks at him, surprised. "Naina? But didn't you always say your favourite name was Mriganayani? That, if you ever had a daughter, you'd call her by that name?"

He sits on his *charpai* and says nothing.

✦

Shakuntala limped slowly across the empty, echoing room, leaving large footprints in the dust. I wish my arthritis would magically disappear so I could come up here more often, she mumbled to herself, running the tip of her index finger on the window ledge and clucking in dismay when it came away grimy. With effort, she reached up to take down the cobwebs hanging from corner to corner, like a delicate net of gold. Then she dragged her bucket of soap water into the furthest corner of the room and, bending as much as her waistline would allow, started mopping the floor one tile at a time.

It took her the better part of two hours to clean the floor, dust the ledges and wipe the walls. Afterwards, she went downstairs to fetch the brown paper packet she had instructed the milkman to deliver earlier that morning. Then she went into the storeroom to collect Sikandar's brass urns, the urns that, unknown to Naina, she polished periodically. Climbing up the stairs again, her arms full, she placed the urns in the two corners of Sikandar's room. Then, unwrapping the packet, she took out six long-stemmed roses – such godless times, when people have to buy flowers from the market instead of being able to pick them in public gardens, she grumbled – and arranged them in the urns.

Sikandar, Sikandar, she said, while tears freely coursed down her cheeks. I miss you so much, Bhai.

I don't know why Deborah's daughter was here, but I didn't tell her anything, Shakuntala whispered. I didn't let your memory be sullied in the eyes of Naina, that silly child who worships you. Besides, this girl Megan seems to love her father. And the two girls have become friends too...so beautiful, both of them. What is the point in raking up a rotten past now? No, the truth will remain with me. Rest in peace, Bhai; the courtesans of Karim Street can keep a secret.

Sitting in a corner of that room, Shakuntala rocked herself gently while the sweet fragrance of roses wafted over her like a blessing. So many people, so many stories...so many hours passing by, until the afternoon light turned sallow. Soon the watery winter sun had dribbled away completely, leaving only tired blue shadows in its wake.

It was the doorbell that jolted Shakuntala out of her reverie. That must be Naina back from the airport, she thought, pulling herself up with great effort. Casting one last look around the room, she limped out, locking the door behind her. Down the stairs, across the courtyard. "Coming, coming," she called, "and *stop* ringing that cursed bell, *ladki*!"

"What took you so long?" Naina asked, walking into the courtyard and bolting the gate. "I was beginning to worry."

"Don't. Your Bua's bones will live through many such winters," Shakuntala replied gruffly, peering into Naina's face. The girl's eyes were red, the lids puffy. "Have you been crying?" Shakuntala asked suspiciously.

Naina nodded. "Megan and I...we both got a little sentimental," she said, embarrassed. Walking into the house, she pushed open the door of her bedroom and flung her bag on the bed.

"Don't speak of that girl! The wretch! She will rot in her plane," Shakuntala shouted, following Naina into her room. "Did she even come to say goodbye to me? Did she?"

Naina smiled. "She has sent you a letter."

"She has? What does it say?"

"I don't know," Naina confessed. "She asked me to wait until I got back home, and to give it to you."

"Ah. A good girl, that Megan," Shakuntala beamed. "At least she is paying her respect to elders. Show, show."

Naina took the envelope out of her bag. "But listen, it will be in English..."

"Again English, English, I am tired of English," Shakuntala shouted. "Everyone, everywhere, just English! Are we living in Delhi or London? Okay, you read it."

The writing was a little faint, the letters flowery and running into each other. Naina switched on the table-lamp and held the sheet of paper under it.

Dear Bua,

It was very nice to meet you. I am sorry I could not come and say goodbye before I left. But I am confident I shall visit India again, so I look forward to meeting you then. And I hope that someday, you and Naina will visit America.

Another thing. Many years ago, your brother gave my mother a gift of a box of jewels. It was a very generous gift, exchanged between two dear friends, but my father and I both believe that the jewels rightfully belong to your family. In fact, I fully expected you and Naina to bring it up during our conversations, and was surprised and touched that you didn't. I did not carry the jewels with me on this trip for obvious reasons, but will be making the necessary arrangements to have them shipped to you safely as soon as I reach America.

The only request I have is that you allow me to keep one piece of jewellery from the box, as a memory of my mother and as a blessing from your brother. I have already decided what I want to keep. The silver anklets, the ones that Rukhsana Jan was wearing the evening she met her prince Roshan. In any case, I love to dance, and I hope that one day the anklets will inspire me to learn Kathak in the old tradition of the courtesans.

Stay well. I will miss you and Naina,

Love,

Megan

Home

It was good to be back. Megan wheeled her luggage out of the airport and looked around. It had snowed continuously on the east coast for the past week and everything was frozen solid, cars like giant white mounds in the parking lots, icy clumps of trees, the air frosty. Glancing at her watch, she flagged down a cab. The Liberty International Airport was in Newark, just fifteen minutes away from her own apartment, but she was going to her father's house in Pennington.

"At least two hours, miss," the cab driver said, apologetically, through the rearview mirror. "New Year's Eve."

"No worries. I've been flying for fifteen hours and that takes a toll, I'll tell you *that*, but I'm not nearly as exhausted as I thought I'd be." It was true. She'd eaten a hearty meal on-board, watched a movie and gone to sleep for a full eight hours, waking up only when the steward had started distributing immigration forms and announcing onward flight information. The way back had somehow been easier.

"We had a white Christmas this year," the driver continued chattily.

"Yes, I can tell. Too bad I missed it," she replied. She'd been in Delhi on Christmas Day this year, and had enjoyed the complimentary cake and mulled cider sent up by the hotel. And the evening before, she'd sauntered around in south Delhi looking at some of the shops and decorations. It had been nice but lonely, and nothing like a dazzling white Christmas in New York City, the streets full of people in furs and boots, the windows of departmental stores dressed with Santas and nativity scenes, colourful signs everywhere, and music, and fairy lights blinking in the trees.

Settling back against her seat and watching the familiar roads flash past, she felt strangely at peace. Beyond the first acute hours of shock, on her last evening in India, her mind had begun to empty itself of its unhappiness. If she could have chosen one parent, she would have chosen her father; of this, she had no doubt. That the choice had been taken out of her hands had actually made things easier. If it was Dad who had cheated on Mother, if he had been the one to have a child with another woman, she would have been upset with him, so upset. But it was Mother who had had the affair more than thirty years ago, the mother whom she didn't even know well enough to call Mom, the mother who had always been just a distant apparition and no more. For how long could one be angry with an apparition?

As for her Dad, Megan had decided that there could only be one of two possibilities: either he had learned, or at least guessed, the truth at some point in his life, or he hadn't. If he already knew, it would only embarrass him further to know his daughter knew too; and if he didn't know, it would be painful, humiliating for him to find out. Either way, nothing would change, not his wife's infidelity in the past nor his daughter's love for him in the present. So there was really no point speaking to her father, Megan had decided. For her father he was, regardless of the calculus of biology and birth; Megan Adams' father *was* Stanley Adams. That other man, Sikandar, with all the good qualities in the world, was still just that other man, a stranger. What an irony it was, she'd thought in her hotel room, that she should stumble upon the truth only after she'd almost given up her quest for it. But standing in the queue for immigration check, shortly after having said her goodbyes to Naina and Shekhar, she'd thought it so befitting that the truth be revealed to her only *after* she'd realised that it was entirely unimportant.

She still wondered about who'd sent that anonymous letter. Back in India, she'd been convinced it was Angela. Angela, who, in Stanley's words, had been quite taken with the new house and had spent a lot of time exploring its nooks; Angela, who could easily have come upon Debbie's diary or some such; Angela, who had learnt a scandalous family truth and didn't know how to handle it. But now, sitting in the cab on her way to see her father on New Year's Eve, Megan realised that the letter could just as well have been sent by any among at least a dozen other people. Guests to her father's house, doctors, friends, neighbours, even the packers who'd helped him move—anyone who had come across the incriminating information and decided to have a little fun with it. Megan could either spend the rest of her winter vacation asking a hundred questions and trying to chase down a nameless culprit, or she could try to put it behind her. I will try to put it behind me, Megan decided. It will not be easy, but I will try.

The signs on the road were a blur. "Where are we?" she asked the cab driver groggily. "I seem to be losing my bearings."

"Just passed New Brunswick," he replied cheerfully. "Pennington is forty five minutes away. You'll soon be home."

✦

Stanley stood in the garden in his boots and gloves. It had been a bitter winter, miles of knee-deep snow, its bottom layers icy and intemperate, the fresh top layer drifting about like sand. It was almost eight in the evening, and the snow glittered in the moonlight like powdered diamonds. And such silence all around, rising from the fields and the empty farmhouses and the frozen river beyond. He looked at the pine trees huddled close, like family. I hope the kid's reached home safely, he thought.

Walking on the pathway he'd shovelled earlier that evening, he couldn't help feeling uneasy. It was a feeling he'd experienced often, ever since Megan had brought up India a few months ago, but he'd told himself he was doing the right thing by letting her go there. The day she left for Delhi, he'd battled the quiet, clotted feeling in his heart for hours. Over the next week, that feeling had come and gone. Sometimes he'd felt completely fine; at other times, his chest had tightened and he'd found himself a little short of breath. The day he'd finally relaxed a bit was the day Megan had called from Delhi and mentioned, in passing, that she had met Shakuntala, and that Shakuntala's brother Sikandar had died several years back.

Stanley hadn't known Sikandar was dead. Such irony that Debbie and Sikandar should both have gone. And such hope, Stanley had thought, with an increasing lift of his heart. For, if Sikandar was dead, there was no way Megan could find out he had been her biological father. Today Megan was returning to America. Let everything be as it was, as it should be, he found himself praying.

Of course he knew. Debbie had told him the same day *she* learned of her pregnancy. Stanley still remembered that day so vividly, the moist heat of an Indian summer, the garden still wet from the previous night's rain, Debbie's tears.

"Do you love him?" he had asked her.

"No, no," she'd answered wretchedly, her face blotchy from crying. "Sikandar is a beautiful human being, a good friend, but no. In fact, even the afternoon we…were together, I was thinking of you, only of you. Please believe me, Stan," she'd wept.

He had walked away from her, his face set in stone. It had been an angry, unslept night for both of them, he pacing the floor of his study while she sat up and sobbed in their bedroom. Up until midnight, his bitterness had rubbed against him like a rock of salt, his jaw hardening at the thought of all that he had done for her, all the countries he had taken her to, the beautiful clothes, and classy dinners, and the *respect*, for God's sake, the respect that she got from the world just from being his wife.

But by the time dawn crept tiredly up the balcony of their house, the gardener turning the hosepipe on the rows of hedges in the garden below and the smell of wet earth rising up to meet him, Stanley had found himself thinking of other things. Like all the mornings he read his newspaper at the breakfast table, impatiently brushing her aside when she tried to talk. Like all the evenings she dressed up for him, pretty clothes and flowers tucked in her hair, and he was too absentminded to notice. "How did I look today?" she had asked him countless times, and he'd looked upon her childlike face with exasperation. Like all the nights when she turned to him and he, tired or preoccupied, pushed her away. Maybe he didn't cheat *on* her with other women, Stanley had thought, but he cheated her all right. His Debbie, who had been abandoned as a baby and grown up in foster homes, and whom he had promised to love, honour and cherish till death did them part…

He'd walked into their bedroom to find her sitting by the window nursing a cup of tea. Her cheeks were streaked, her hair dishevelled, her nose red. She'd never looked more beautiful. "Give me a divorce, Stan," she'd said flatly, not looking at him. "Just have the papers served. I won't contest it, or ask for anything."

"I don't want the details. But how…often did you…?" he'd murmured, unable to help himself. "I mean…with him?"

"Just once. Just that one time. I haven't seen him since."

"Why didn't you tell me then?"

"I tried to, several times. Couldn't. But after I took the pregnancy test, I…had to. I couldn't pretend the baby was yours, I just couldn't."

"Do you still love me?" he'd asked then.

"Of course," she'd said, starting to cry all over again. And she'd got up and run to him, snuggling her face in the crook of his neck and smelling his skin like she used to when they first got married. "I've missed you, missed you so much," she'd sobbed. "I'll get an abortion."

"You don't need to, unless you want to. This child will be ours. Everything will be fine," he'd said, running his fingers through her hair. "I have a plan. Let's go back to America, Debbie. Let's go home."

And they had. Come back home. Stanley had put in his papers with the government and taken up a job at the United Nations Headquarters in New York City, along with a consulting position for a political think-tank in Washington, DC. Since Debbie felt daunted by the thought of raising a family in a large city, they'd decided to live in the beautiful, historical town of Princeton. That's where the children had been born, first Megan, then Jeff. And they'd been happy, very happy.

He still wondered why it didn't last longer, why it wasn't enough to keep those shadows away from under her eyes and the emptiness from their green pooling depths. It had been so hard for him to see the raw ache inside her dry up and turn into a dead, peeling thing, her whole life a blister, her slow return to a world of fantasy, from which she'd slipped in and out, in and out...

After Debbie died, it hadn't taken him too long to learn how to be a single dad. Maybe it was because his children were special, and had made it all so easy—Jeff, more serious and withdrawn, a little man even at five, and Megan, unrestrained, full of life, always laughing. Birthdays, proms, heartbreaks, graduations, jobs—how the children had grown, the years piling one on top of the other, some downs, mostly ups, a full life...until this whole India business sprung up from nowhere.

He wondered what Megan had been hiding from him. She'd clearly learned something, but he didn't know what it was, or from where. After Debbie died, he'd destroyed all her diaries, if only because he didn't want the children to read anything disturbing. But that was in their Princeton house, years back...was it possible that some secrets had survived amid the stacks of books and papers, secrets as small and wingless as silverfish, and as damaging?

Stanley looked at the pile of snow on top of the birdhouse and exhaled deeply. I must drag the ladder here and knock off some of that snow tomorrow, he thought. And I will get more seeds for the poor little birds, how their eyes dart about hungrily the whole day, their beaks picking at the frozen ground. I will build a tiny shelter for the squirrels and their babies tomorrow. Tomorrow I will call Megan.

Stanley took a last look around his garden and turned to go inside the house. On the steps, he scraped the snow off his boots and was just about to switch off the lights on the porch when the sound of a car made him turn around again. Sure enough, there it was, emerging through the blackness of the trees, its headlights like two circles of sun. And it was rolling up into his driveway, and there was Megan!

"Dad!" she yelled, pulling her suitcase out and grinning like a monkey.

"What are you doing here? Didn't you go to your apartment?" Stanley called out delightedly, clambering down the stairs again and almost running up the pathway.

"Nope. Wanted to come see you, spend the last week of my winter vacation here," she said, paying off the cab driver and helping him reverse. After the cab had driven off, she started trundling up to the house with her luggage.

"Give your stuff to me," he said, slightly out of breath.

"Relax, Dad. And why were you *running*? You could have tripped," she mock-scolded him. "Brrr, it's freezing out here. Let's get inside already. But first, a hug."

"I missed you, Meg," he said, hugging her, the tip of her nose cold like it always used to be, even as a child. She was blabbering about her India trip, and about some girl and her aunt and a mountain and a chef and an old city and a new city, but for once, Stanley couldn't care less. The only thing he cared about was that she was his daughter, and that she was home.

✦

I can't believe how the winter break just flew past, Megan ruminated, distributing copies of her syllabus on American women writers. It was the second week of January and the first day of the spring term in the university, rows of new faces in every class. The students leafed through the pages of the syllabus noisily. After class ended, some of those syllabi would end up soaring and reaching new heights as paper planes, Megan thought with a smile.

"So the course will examine canonical literary texts from a variety of critical perspectives. Feminist, Marxist, existential, psychoanalytical, postcolonial.... And notice the blank days towards the end of the syllabus? That will be our little experiment," Megan said, eyes twinkling. "I want us to see if there can be multiple, even diametrically opposite, ways of reading the *same* text."

"That makes sense, the multiple ways thing," a girl in the front row interjected. "It's so frustrating when people argue about the *one* right way to think. I mean, this isn't math! And, well, if they are all saying different things, how can they all be right anyway?"

Megan laughed. "Yes, this is not math. So let's move away from true and false, right and wrong. Instead, keep a broad mind, be open to different ways of seeing things. Ask whether or not it is a convincing argument, that's what I say."

"Yes, but the problem is that they all sound convincing," one of the boys said. "I was taking a political theory course last term. Each time we read a new book and got convinced of its thesis, along came another book to convince us otherwise. It was so crazy. I didn't know *what* to believe!"

Before Megan could answer, a voice shot out from the back row. "Don't sweat it, man, believe whatever makes you happy."

That could be one way, Megan mused. That, as pasts and presents meld, and histories and cultures collide, truth becomes what each of us makes of it. Truth shimmers and shifts from moment to moment; truth is what makes us happy. Aloud, she said, "Well, that's exactly the point of education. To have you know less and less, rather than more and more."

"What do you mean?" someone asked.

"It goes like this, guys," Megan said with a grin. "When you think you have all the answers, they give you your high school degree. When you realise you *don't* have all the answers, they give you the undergrad. And when you realise neither does anyone else, you'll finally get your graduate degree."

The class laughed, and Megan laughed along. She knew it would be another term of challenges. Of indiscipline, anxiety, indifference. Oh, they would stumble, slip up here, take a wrong turn there... Sometimes they would lose hope, and courage, and faith—and sometimes she would. But there would be more success than failure, for her students *and* for her; of this she was confident, and she couldn't wait to get started.

After the class had ended and students had vacated the room noisily, Megan began to collect her papers.

"Excuse me, Miss."

Megan looked up to see a tall girl in a cardigan, denim skirt and thigh-high boots. "Yes?"

"My name is Violet, Miss. My brother, he was in your class," the girl said earnestly. She had a stunning figure and a mole on her chin.

"It's the first day of class, and I don't yet know my students well..." Megan said, wondering why the girl looked familiar.

"No, no, I meant he was in your class in the fall. Derek. He was always speaking of you at home, he was," she said. "Saying your course really made him think."

"Ah yes, Derek, of course," Megan said, remembering the shy teenager who hardly spoke in class, but who had impressed her with his well-researched written assignments. "How is he doing?"

"We...we had some issues with paying the spring tuition, so he had to register late," she said, shifting her weight from one foot to the other. "Now all the classes he wants to get into are full, yours too. I says let me go speak to your professors, he says Violet back off, but I came."

Megan smiled at her. "I'm glad you did, Violet, and it's not a problem at all. Once I get back home, I will e-mail him a special permission number which he can use to register."

"You will?" she said, her face lighting up. "That's great! We aren't rich, Miss. Derek, he works part-time mornings and goes to school afternoons, and me, I work part-time nights and go to school mornings."

"I'm so happy to hear you're both getting an education. Looks like you are making all the right choices."

The girl bit her lip. "I won't lie to you, Miss. I am an exotic dancer at a gentleman's club. Don't like to be called stripper, so demeaning. It's a job too, I say, it pays the bills. But I want to get out soon. I'm making good grades, and once I get my college degree, I can apply for a nice job."

As Violet was speaking, it suddenly came back to Megan in a rush: the neon lights, she and Kevin parked outside Karim's, the goddess of the night—mole, mini-skirt and purple printed tights. Was this the same girl? But that had been long ago, and it was hard to tell for sure. "I'm done for the day," Megan said. "Would you like to walk with me to Broad Street?"

"Sure," Violet said, looking thrilled. "Wait till I tell Derek I was hanging out with you!"

They walked out of the classroom, through the foyer and out of the building. The afternoon was icy: sludge on the sidewalks, skiddy streets, fresh snow swirling down continuously. "Are you originally from Newark?" Megan asked Violet while slipping on her gloves.

"Yeah, I was born here. This city has changed so much. My parents say it used to be a lot better but then there was a slump, and some say it's still on. But I say it's getting better."

"You think so?"

"Totally. Less violence, less drugs on the street. And this place is so *happy*. Some other streets in some other cities are so stuffy, everyone sayin' and doin' the right thing and whatnot, but this, this place I love!"

Megan turned to Violet in surprise, but the girl was busy smiling at all the passers-by and showing her middle finger to a man who'd leered at her. Grinning, Megan looked ahead again, seeing the snow-covered city through Violet's eyes, the new restaurants and pizzerias, the colourful wigs shops, the polytechnic just round the corner advertising courses for the new session, two teenagers sprinting down the street.

"Okay, Violet, I live just across from here, so I'll say goodbye to you now," she said, once they had reached the Broad Street intersection. "It was very nice meeting you. Do come see me again. And I'll look forward to seeing Derek in class."

"It was real nice meeting you too, Miss. And…just so you know, I haven't told Derek about the exotic dancer thing," she said, looking discomfited. "I won't be doing it for very long anyway, so no point telling him, I says. Don't snitch on me, please."

"Don't worry, I won't," Megan said with a smile.

The courtesans of Karim Street can keep a secret.

Friends

Naina took off her sandals and walked barefoot on the lush, springy grass, under the drooping boughs of the Amaltas trees. It was the end of March, the freezing winter months far behind, flowers in full bloom, here and there a laden fruit tree. An early evening sun scattered bursts of diamond light, and, through the leaves and the branches, peeked the lake's golden shimmer.

She looked at her watch. Shekhar would be here any minute, she thought, smiling at the memories of the past few months. He'd filled her days with so much joy and warmth and richness, even though they'd never done anything expensive together. Instead, they had wandered through the narrow streets of the old city and the wider ones of the new. They'd browsed books in nooky stores, *kulhad*s of steaming hot tea in hand. They'd sat cross-legged on the floor, in 'free to the public' classical music concerts, watched birds at sunrise, learned the names of the trees in new neighbourhoods, laughed together, on the silted banks of the Yamuna, and held hands in sadness to see its polluted, pewter-coloured water. That is why today's conversation would be so hard.

When she saw his lean, boyish form emerging through the faraway line of trees, her heart skipped a beat.

"I will take you out for dinner tonight, to celebrate. Some *really* fancy place, and I won't hear any no's," he said with enthusiasm, once he'd joined her. "An arts fellowship in America! I've been so proud since you gave me the news last night I couldn't even sleep."

She nodded, not meeting his eyes. "I couldn't either."

He looked at her profile, his broad smile slowly shading into concern. "What's the matter? I thought you would be... oh no. No, Naina, no, we don't need to! So many people have long-distance relationships..."

That was when she turned towards him, her eyes unslept. "It's so uncanny," she said softly, laying a hand on his shoulder, "the way you can always guess what is on my mind."

"Is that why you called me?" he demanded, raising her chin so she could look at him squarely in the eyes. "To end our relationship?"

"You don't understand," she said sadly.

"Try explaining your point. I'm listening. I thought we were happy, Naina."

"Happy, yes. Very. But I never could forget the difference in our backgrounds..."

"Stop that, just stop it," he cut in. "Have I ever cared about that? Did you ever feel I was judging you? That is ridiculous!"

"For you, maybe, but what about your parents?" she asked, her tone gentle. "What about Neelima Aunty? For her, I must be this girl who first tried to get her hooks into her son and now his friend..."

"*Neelima Aunty*? I am supposed to care about what *she* thinks? And why is all this even coming up? You're breaking up because of the fellowship, because you are going away, and not because of the disparity in our backgrounds! And the disparity thing is bullshit, by the way—Megan's family has returned your jewels, you are getting your haveli renovated, you don't even *have* serious money problems anymore!"

"That's true," Naina admitted. "When I decided to apply for the fellowship, I didn't know we would get our jewels back. I wanted to stop worrying about the electricity bills, the home repairs.... But it wasn't only about money, you know that. I wanted to dance, make something of myself."

"And didn't I support your decision? Didn't I help you with your applications? Didn't I? And once you get accepted, you want to break up with me because of the difference in our *backgrounds*! You know what? I don't even want to have this conversation," Shekhar said hotly, turning and starting to walk away.

"Shekhar, please, please don't go away like this," she implored, running after him. "The two things are related, can't you see?" she asked, her eyes watering. "This fellowship removes some of the differences between us, makes people stop talking. But if we are still together, I won't be able to go! When I was applying, I didn't think I'd get accepted, I really didn't. But now...and even if I go, all I will do is keep thinking of you, and missing you, and wanting to come back."

"What you are saying doesn't even make *sense*, you know that?" Shekhar asked, frustrated. "You are saying you want to be with me, that you want my family to be proud of you, but that you *don't* want to be with me! And will you please stop crying?" He pulled her close and wiped her cheeks tenderly. "What do you want?"

"I want to be with you. But I also want to be proud of myself, and you to be proud of me. I don't want to give up this chance," she said, snuggling close and smelling the clean, fresh scent of him.

"Have I stopped you?" he asked, wrapping his arms tight around her.

"No, but it will be difficult for me to go if we are still together. I will constantly think of you, I know I will. And I can't even ask *you* to come with me," she said sadly. "I know how passionate you are about the historical preservation work you want to do in India. Heritage buildings, the old city..."

"Go with you? Wait, does this mean you are thinking of *settling* abroad?"

"Of course not!" Naina replied impatiently. "Just a couple of years. And you know me, my roots, everything. This is just a way to...do well."

"Do well. Right. As if people don't do well here," Shekhar said, bitter for once. "I've not said this before, but do you really think it's going to be a cakewalk abroad? No discrimination, an equal world—where you fit right in?"

"I've never lived in an equal world," Naina said quietly. "I've never fit in. Not with my own people, not with yours. Even now I'm scared."

"Then don't go," he said impulsively.

"No. I want to see new places, make new friends, dance. I have hope. If we don't have hope, Shekhar, what do we have?"

"And for that, you want to end our relationship!"

"It doesn't have to be forever. Afterwards..."

Shekhar was quiet. "I don't know what to do," he said, his voice heavy.

"It's all my fault. I'll never forgive myself for causing you, us, this pain..."

"*Kee mere qatl ke baad usne jafaa se tauba, Hae us zuud-pashiimaan ka pashiimaan hona*. When will you be leaving?"

"Sometime in August, I think," she whispered, not wanting to think about it.

"Then why do we have to end things now? It's only March," he muttered, wanting a month, a week, a day, even just an hour more.

"The longer we wait, the harder it will be," she said, fresh tears rolling down her cheeks. "Now we can go back to our lives...I have to finalise the renovations, make arrangements for Bua, bank accounts, passport, visa. And you, you can focus on—"

"Never mind what I can focus on!" Shekhar said roughly, his own eyes wet.

They stood holding each other for a long, long time, oblivious to the hoots and horns of vehicles on the road, the stares of passers-by and groups of giggling schoolchildren, while the evening shed its orange overcoat and shrugged on the star-spangled negligee of night. "Can I still take you out for dinner?" Shekhar asked, running his fingers through her hair.

She smiled through her tears. "Yes. To the most outrageously expensive place your father's money can buy," she said, making him smile too.

"If we feel the same way about each other a couple of years later as we do now, we can get back together again, right?" he asked, sighing in relief when Naina nodded. "And till then, we can at least be friends?" he persisted.

"Of course," Naina replied, reaching for his hand and lacing her fingers through his. "My best friend."

Stillness fell upon them, as weighty as a promise. The two of them walked in silence, along the still, moonlit landscape, and through the drowsing trees.

✦

Shakuntala flung all her clothes into a large steel trunk, cursing under her breath. "Better if you had collapsed and taken me with you," she muttered in Hindi, looking up and glaring at the ceiling. "Now only I will collapse. You will get a fancy renovation, and everyone will have *biryani* and *sewaiyan* to celebrate, but I won't be there to see all the revelry! Because I will have died from all this work!"

That good girl Megan had been true to her promise and sent the jewels. Afterwards, Naina, idealistic as always: no, Bua, we won't sell them, they are family heirlooms, the only reminders of the glory of Karim Street. But aunt's sense had prevailed over niece's sentimentality. Most of the jewels had been sold, two-thirds of the money safely in a fixed deposit and the remaining one-third going towards renovating the haveli. The construction workers came every day now, with steel rods and baked brick and cement, tearing down partitions and walls, spraying chemicals, kicking up horse-hooves of dust.

If only I had known the renovation would mean so much work for me – packing, moving things from one room to the other, fetching this and that for the workers – maybe I would have let Naina hold on to the jewels, and this haveli be damned, Shankuntala now thought, pulling her clothes out of their shelves with a vengeance. Why, just this morning, one of the workers had had the audacity to lie on her *charpai* in the courtyard and asked her to fetch him a glass of water! "There is a ditch flowing just outside this house; go and drink from there," she had told him with an imperial wag of her index finger. Still, it was good that the haveli would be restored to some of its former glory, she thought. Sikandar, God bless his soul, would be happy wherever he was, and Naina would be able to leave her worries behind when she left for America.

Ah, America. Wait till the neighbours hear of this, Shakuntala smirked. Ever since the acceptance letter had arrived from the Arts Foundation yesterday, Shakuntala had been imagining herself in scandalous clothes, loitering in Los Angeles and having wild evenings in Vegas. "Your passport this, your passport that. When are you getting *my* passport done?" she had finally demanded, a hand on her hip.

"You can't go right away, Bua. First I must settle in, and only then will I take you for a trip," Naina had firmly announced, smiling when her aunt flounced around grumpily. "Don't worry. There's the monthly interest from the fixed deposit. And I will write to you regularly."

"Will you buy me contacs so I can read your letters?" Shakuntala had asked hopefully, making Naina burst into peals of laughter.

"Yes, Bua, I will. I know you don't want glasses because they make you look old. Contact lenses for you this week itself."

So all was well, Shakuntala thought, pulling out her old albums from their moth-balled top shelf in the cupboard. The sorrows of the past erased, the future filled with joy, and God bless the courtesans.

Wiping her face with her dupatta, Shakuntala sat down on her bed and began thumbing through one of the albums. There they all were, brought instantly to life by the turn of a page—Amma, shrewd-eyed and double-chinned, golden boy Sikandar and his sweet wife, so many others, friends, neighbours...and she. Drawing in a deep breath, Shakuntala looked at the only photograph of Debbie she had. Hatted, hand-bagged, sunglassed Debbie, with her emerald eyes and sunshine smile.

The photograph had been taken by Sikandar, with their father's British-era camera. As she squinted at the sepia picture with its sunburned throng of tourists milling around Debbie, and in the background the rising ramparts of the Red Fort, Shakuntala recalled what Debbie had said to her, just before she'd left their lives: I will always think of you as my friend, Shakuntala. Always.

"Okay. Friends," she said gruffly, kissing Debbie's old photograph.

✦

"How time flies," Stanley remarked, taking a sip from his morning cup of coffee. He and Megan were sitting on the porch and looking at the magnolia bush in front of the garage. Sated from its winter slumber, the solitary bush had awoken to April, that month of excess, of sunbeams and sudden colours.

During his most recent visit, Jeff had remarked on its ungenerous location – a single bush, and that too entirely invisible from the road, he'd said – but for father and daughter, this made the magnolia bush a private joy, and all the more enchanting.

"Yes." Megan turned to smile at her father. "Five months ago, it was winter, everything bare. And I was in India."

"A long winter," Stanley said softly.

"But now it's spring," Megan countered, squeezing his hand.

"Yes, it is. So tell me, did your friend Naina write again? After last week's e-mail, I mean."

"No. She's probably busy with the renovations in their house, and all her paperwork."

"When is she coming here?"

"The position begins in September, so sometime in August I suppose."

"You don't look too happy," Stanley remarked astutely. "I should have thought you'd be more excited."

Megan sighed. "I *am* excited for her. I feel proud—and thrilled we'll be able to hang out again."

"But…?" Stanley prompted.

"I wish her relationship with Shekhar had worked out. The two of them had something special. Don't know why she had to call that off…and why are *you* grinning?"

"Well, because of the irony of it," Stanley replied, his eyes twinkling. "She was this traditional girl who wanted marriage, and you wanted to focus on work, work. And now she's the one walking away from her guy to pursue her professional ambitions, and you're the one postponing all career decisions in order to get hitched! It's kinda funny if you think about it."

"Stop it," Megan muttered. "Things with me and Kevin aren't *certain* the way you're assuming."

"Right." Stanley teased, laughing uproariously when she glared.

"I'm serious. I'm still trying to work everything out so we're each free to make the right decisions. I must let Kevin get on with his life, his dreams, instead of having to start a family right away. And I…I haven't stopped wanting to write books, or teach, or do a postdoc, or a zillion other things. I'm still me.

"Well. The boy is on his way back from Beijing, isn't he?"

"Yes. He's probably boarding his flight even as we speak."

"Good, good." Stanley took another sip of his coffee.

It had rained the previous night: damp earth, the imprint of deer hooves everywhere. After the deer had uprooted a bush and eaten some of the flowers last week, he'd fenced in his precious lily bulbs and taped the young barks of the trees. Now everything was growing as it should, the lilies, the violets, the saplings he had planted earlier in the year so sprightly, the saw grass stacked in dry bunches slowly turning tall and green. It really was a beautiful spring.

They sat around and chatted for a little while longer. Later, Stanley went back inside to do the laundry and Megan decided to take a little walk in the grounds. Everything was vibrant now, the flowers, the dense bursts of leaves in so many shades of green, lime and olive, the grass spangled with violets, the pine trees tall and gentlemanly, cones clinging to their lips like pipes. Her father had chopped and arranged logs of wood in high piles for next winter, and Megan smiled to see two squirrels play on the top log. A difficult year ending on such a happy, happy note, Megan thought, looking at an orange butterfly that had settled upon the magnolia bush. In that soundless, secluded world, amid the flowers, trees, thicket and bracken, amid the squirrel and the deer and the butterfly, she suddenly felt blessed.

It would be hard to describe afterwards, but for a moment, it seemed to Megan like her mother was telling her she loved her. The mother she knew so little about, the mother she had never been able to understand. As Megan stared at the magnolia bush in surprise and confusion, the orange butterfly spread its spangled wings and soared higher, higher, reaching up into the heavens and out of sight.

Excerpts from a Diary

The magnolia is a beautiful flower: white, pink-tipped, partial to the sun. It looks like an exquisitely crafted work of origami, its flowers like large, exotic birds preparing for flight. From my bedroom window, I look down at the magnolia bushes growing in the garden, and at the pink blush slowly creeping up the sky's neckline. It is a beautiful spring day and I should be happy, but I am not. Sighing, I turn around and walk back to my bed where my diary lies face-down. Propping myself against my pillows, I pick up my pen again.

Happiness, a skill I never learnt. Is it genetic? Did I have unhappy parents? I don't know. Most children in foster care have files; teenage mothers who gave them up for adoption, junkie fathers who bolted. I was a baby left on the steps of the church and discovered by the mailman; I was file-less and free. My first foster home had a large garden and there was a strong smell of soil, everywhere soil. Years later, I would only remember the garden and the soil and its raw, mealy smell; the people I would forget. In my second foster home, the rooms were dark and my new father had a smile I did not like. He wanted to dress me and undress me, dress me and undress me. My new mother watched and cried. I ran away from the third and fourth homes; I was a wild-child, a beast. The fifth was finally different; the woman was old, widowed and childless until she adopted me. She sang to me like a mother, a grandmother, haunting songs of lost lands that filled me up. She had a lovely voice, so full of care, but maybe it was too late.

I took long walks in the meadows. I grew up. I learned to smile at people, to converse about nothing at all. In my senior year of high school, I was Prom Queen; in my senior year of college, I was chased by the boys. They all said I'm beautiful. But when I looked in the mirror, I imagined scars, so many scars. I always wore make-up.

After college, another crossroad: my foster-mother died, leaving everything to me. Our townhouse in the city, a small cottage in the country, enough money in the bank. It was so tempting, the urge to escape into those houses full of rooms, the townhouse's musty, moth-eaten library, the cottage scullery and kitchen. To stick to those walls like plaster, to have the hardwood floors grow on me like skin…but no, I said to myself. I must embrace the teeming life of this world…to wear the change of seasons lightly, like perfume…to breathe in the sun. I can't keep running away, I just can't. Then I saw an advertisement in the local newspaper, about the governor's office looking to staff some temporary positions. Temporary, a word unburdened and uplifting, an anywhere word. Oh, I can be a temp, I thought with relief.

It was in that office, sitting in my tiny cubicle with a desk, a stack of papers and a potted plant, that I met Stanley. He was a career diplomat, an old friend of the Governor's. Stanley was ten years older than me, not classically handsome but very distinguished-looking. When our eyes met, he appeared to hesitate for only a second before striding towards me confidently. "Lunch?" he asked, looking at his watch.

It was a whirlwind courtship, Stanley such a gentleman: flowers, dinners, concerts. Within six months, we were married. It is still so vivid in my memory, the day we exchanged our vows: the white of the wedding cake, my pearly white gown, our white dazzling hopes. We went to the Caribbean for a week-long honeymoon, and it was a time of such wild happiness, hotels with pretty balconies, beachfront restaurants, dancing cheek-to-cheek in tune with the turquoise, tumbling music of the waves, foam in our faces, knolls of sand and seashells at our feet.

In those early weeks, we would talk for hours at night while we spooned. I have a home, I have a home, I would murmur; Stan would listen, and smile indulgently. But, like all things good, the honeymoon was soon over. He immersed himself in his work again, and in his travels around the world. Sometimes I accompanied him, and at other times I stayed behind. But that was just geography; together or apart, our lives became an endless litany of lunches, meetings, files, protocol. This is my world, Debbie, and you better get used to it, he began to snap more and more often. Six years passed, with him rising rapidly within the ranks of government, and I hugging my own silences once again, my walks in the meadows, my unpeopled inner world.

And then, India…

Haven't I written about these things already, in my earlier diaries? My foster homes, my meeting Stan, our coming together and growing apart? I cannot remember. There is so much I don't remember these days. Anyway, after we return to America from India, Stan is so caring. He is the man I fell in love with seven years ago, the man I married. But I am not the same woman, for another life grows inside that lifts me up and pulls me down by turn. I do mention divorce one more time;

again, he refuses. He gives up his prestigious job and picks up another one that will not require us to travel. He wants to make our marriage work, and having him tuck me in at night and looking at his hopeful face first thing in the morning, I almost begin to believe it is possible. Then the baby arrives.

When I see her the first time, she is crying, smeared in my blood. She is born of me, of my muscle and tissue. These tiny hands and feet come from me, I marvel. From me and Sikandar, another voice grates inside, and I turn away abruptly. Afterwards, the nurse brings her out, clean, swaddled in white, sleeping peacefully. I see that her skin is slightly darker than mine and Stanley's. The nurse extends her arms towards us: me propped up in the hospital bed, and Stan standing next to me, his arm around my shoulders. I reach out for my bundle, but her wrinkled baby face is turned towards Stan. A few seconds later, she is dimpling prettily in her sleep, her little fists clenched tightly at her chest. He takes her from the nurse and cradles her in his arms. A bond has formed between them, I can see, a bond bigger than blood and birth; from that moment, I am the stranger. "Her eyes are the exact colour as yours…", Stan says excitedly, marvelling at her baby green eyes as she wakes up and blinks in the hard light. They're the Karim Street eyes, I think dully.

"What do you want to call her?" the nurse asks.

"Megan," I reply, looking away.

Stan thinks I have never hidden anything from him. He is wrong. I have hidden from him the reason for our daughter's name. Stan does not know of Sikandar's stories, told long ago, under the lip of the Amaltas trees, in the light of the fading sun. Stan does not know Sikandar's own favourite, the story of Gwalior's Raja Man Singh Tomar's feisty Gujari queen, Mriganayani.

The first time I had heard Sikandar say that name, it sounded a bit like Megan to me. When I went to see Sikandar that last time in Delhi, to tell him the truth about my pregnancy and to bid him goodbye, he asked me if it was a boy or a girl, his eyes so gentle and full of pain it broke my heart.

"Seems like it's a girl, but they can't know for sure since it's just about twelve weeks," I replied.

"I know it will be a girl," he said quietly.

I didn't ask him how he knew. Everything about Sikandar spoke of the still wisdoms that lie buried in the womb of the earth and that science cannot explain; I took this as yet another instance of his deep, deep soul. That's when he gave me the jewels—except that I didn't know what the box held at the time.

"For my daughter," he said softly.

I never met Sikandar again. I did call him once, frantically, right after I opened the box and saw the jewels. But no matter how much I begged and pleaded, he refused to take them back. For my daughter, he said again. Well, if it is a daughter, I will call her Megan, I promised Sikandar, smiling through my tears.

In the years that followed, this name sat inside me like sour metal, its iron turning my heart black. Each time Stan called our daughter – Megan, Meg, he said, holding his arms open for her and she bounded into them, first as a tubby, tottering baby and later, on slimmer, surer legs as she learnt to walk and run – I died a little more. When Jeff was born exactly three years after Megan's birth, I assumed things might change. But no; Stan loved Jeff, for sure, yet his love for his own son could never dampen his always-a-little-extra love for another man's daughter.

I think it would have been easier for me if Stan hadn't loved Megan so much. I would have defended myself and my choices, stepped in as her mother, and loved her as mine. Stan's forgiveness robbed me of even that. Stan does not blame me, and so I must blame myself. The doctors have called it depression and a dozen other names, this syndrome, that disorder, my bedside table littered with pills and portions, but I think the names only hint at the husk of an ailment; the inner kernel remains unnamed and intact.

Now Jeff is almost five, Megan about to turn eight. I feel my life slipping away from me, a little more every day, not like something solid being yanked away from under my foot, but something liquidy, molten, more precious, flowing out of me...flying out of my bedroom window and into the hedges, the trees, the undulating expanses of field, the infinite sky. Who am I? What was my purpose? I ask myself again and again, wanting some semblance of an answer before I am gone. I am compulsively filling up the pages of my diaries, past, present and future crammed together in a last-ditch effort to understand.

Afterwards, the black-eyed pages point inky fingers at me. You are a woman loved by two wonderful men, neither of whom you could measure up to, they say. You are a mother who could not love. You could not love, Debbie. Such a cross to bear, such a heavy cross.

I must remember to ask Stan to preserve my diaries, so my daughter can read them someday. Someday, when she is a grown woman, with a woman's heart that has known love, laughter and loss...Megan, if you are reading this when I am no more, please know that I loved you. Oh, I had many flaws and I made mistakes...but if, in trying to make some meaning of the mess that was my life, you decide to take away only one thing, let it be this, my child: I loved you.

I must have been lost in my diary for several hours; it is midday now, and I can see the sun hanging high. Writing has cleansed me, given me new eyes, like it always does. Climbing out of bed and walking to the window, I stick my head out to look at the splendour of spring, at the trees wrapped thick with magenta blossoms, tousles of forsythia, a sweeping dogwood, violets and crocuses in the hedges, clutches of daffodils in every nook.

Suddenly, a silvered joy streaks inside me like lightening, a joy born of the sun, the magnolia, the delicate china sky, the birds, and butterflies, and the unsolved mysteries of motherhood, and my daughter's laughter, and for a brief, brief moment, I am whole again.

Acknowledgements

Every book is a journey, and I am indebted to all those who have travelled with me. To my mother Ratna and my sister Aatreyi, my first and most indulgent readers. To my publishers Bikash and Tultul Niyogi of Niyogi Books, Delhi and to Boxwallah and Renuka Chatterjee, for adopting this book. To Roxie Freeman, my stellar teaching assistant, for the snowy winter evenings spent in my office poring over the edits. To Veena Oldenburg's academic work 'Lifestyle as Resistance: The Case of the Courtesans of Lucknow,' which inspired one of the themes in the book; the onus for liberties taken, in fact and fiction, lies with me. To Gene Adam, whose beautiful home in Pennington, New Jersey, provided such solace! To friends whose journeys have melded with mine, in India, America and elsewhere. To our many pasts, our magical futures. And always, to love.

✦